The Orloj of Paris

The Orloj series: Vol. 3

Erasmus Cromwell-Smith II

The Orloj of Paris
© Erasmus Cromwell-Smith II
© Erasmus Press

ISBN: 978-1-7369968-7-4
Library of Congress Number: Case # 1-11020055631

Publisher: Erasmus Press
Editor: Elisa Arraiz Lucca
Co-Editor: Tracy-Ann Wynter
Proofreading: D. Suster, Tracy-Ann Wynter
Cover Design: Alfredo Sainz Blanco
erasmuscromwellsmith.com
First edition
Printed in USA, 2021.

Books written by the author

In English,
As Erasmus Cromwell-Smith II:

En Español,
Como Erasmus Cromwell-Smith II:

The Equilibrist series,
(Inspirational/Philosophical)
- The Happiness Triangle (Volume 1).
- Geniality (Volume 2).
- The Magic in Life (Volume 3).
- Poetry in Equilibrium (Volume 4).

La serie del Equilibrista,
(Inspiracional/Filosófico)
- El triángulo de la felicidad (Volumen 1).
- Genialidad (Volumen 2).
- La magia de la vida (Volumen 3).
- Poesía en equilibrio (Volumen 4).

(Young Adults)
-The Orloj of Prague (Volume 5).
-The Orloj of Venice (Volume 6).
-The Orloj of Paris (Volume 7).
-The Orloj of London (Volume 8).
- Poetry in Balance (Volume 9).

(Jóvenes Adultos)
- El Orloj de Praga (Volumen 5).
- El Orloj de Venecia (Volumen 6).
- El Orloj de Paris (Volumen 7).
- El Orloj de London (Volumen 8).
- Poesía en Balance (Volumen 9).

As Erasmus Cromwell-Smith

Como Erasmus Cromwell-Smith II

The South Beach Conversational Method
(Educational)
- Spanish
- German
- French
- Italian
- Portuguese

El Método Conversacional South Beach
(Educacional)
- Inglés,
- Alemán
- Francés
- Italiano
- Portugués

The Nicolas Tosh Series, (Sci-fi)
- Algorithm-323 (Volume 1)
- Tosh (Volume 2)

As Nelson Hamel (*)
The Paradise Island Series,
(Action/Thriller)
- Miami Beach, Paradise Island (Volume 1)
- Miami Beach, Dangerous Lifestyles (Volume 2)
- White Spaces at Lake Erie (Volume 1) (Sci/fi)

(*) in collaboration with Charles Sibley.

All titles are or will be available in audio book

Table of Content

Glossary

"Characters"

-The Orloj

-The Burly Man (The street version of The Orloj)

-Thumbpee

-Buggie

"The Six Harlequins"

- Erasmus Jr. aka BLUNT; blue clothes Boston, Mass. USA.
- Sofia aka REDDISH; red clothes, Barcelona, Spain.
- Sanjiv aka FIREE; orange clothes; Mumbai, India.
- Winnie aka CHECKERED; black & white clothes; Pretoria, South Africa.
- Sang-Chang aka BREEZIE; yellow clothes, Shanghai, China.
- Carole aka GREENIE; green clothes, Beirut, Lebanon.

"The Six Sheppard-Moors"

- Cornelius Tetragor, Sheppard-Moor of Honesty; long white hair, ponytail, wears a long robe.
- Lazarus Zeetrikus, Sheppard-Moor of Holding Grudges; a tall old man with a bent old hat.
- Lucrecia Van Egmond, Sheppard-Moor of Perseverance and Grit; long white threaded hair, pale skim aquiline nose, milky blue eyes, fine features, ankle-length skirt, long sleeve shirt.
- Paulina Tetrikus, Sheppard-Moor of Loyalty; short and hunched, short fuse, avoid looking in the eye, beautiful but angry face, short black hair, green eyes.

- Morpheus Rubicom, Sheppard-Moor of Betrayal; nervous, never sits still, puffy eyes, extremely skinny and tall, mat of wrangled curled hair, wears loose-fitting, hanging clothes.
- Lettizia Dilletante, Sheppard-Moor of Forgiveness; blonde hair on a ponytail, statuesque, self-aware but humble. A Nordic beauty with a Mediterranean name.

"Other Characters"
- Erasmus Sr. (Blunt's father).
- Victoria (Blunt's mother).
- Zbynek Kraus, the clock antiquarian. Long white hair in a ponytail, Fumanchu mustache, wears an electric blue robe, and bent cone hat (both with stars and bolts).
- Bartolomeus, Roberto, and Maria Antonella (Blunt's uncles and aunt).
- Antonella D'Agostino & Leonardo Conti (Italian antiquarians).
- Mrs. Victoria Sutton-Raleigh (Mrs. V).

"Powers Earned"
- Each of you now has the power to create an energy shield to protect you. If together, it will be in the form of a domed-shaped shield protecting you all, otherwise each of you would be able to generate a shield in the form of a side plate.
- You all now have the ability to see if people are infected with a virus even through walls you explicitly express the desire to do so.
- You guys now have the ability to connect the dots.
- You all now have the ability to deal with doubt and obtain positive outcomes from uncertainty.
- You now have the ability to sense when danger is approaching you.
- From now on you'll be able to use all your powers on your final six challenges.

In the introductory book of the series "The Orloj of Prague," our magical adventure went on like this...

The very first time I saw The Orloj from afar, across Prague's "Nove Mesto" Square (The Old Town Square); I felt an inexplicable and intense pull seize me. It all took place on a European summer vacation -I was just twelve years old- while strolling along with my parents over the streets of the magical town.

My fascination with the ancient yet resplendent astrological clock led me into an alternate menacing world within the mysterious city of spires; where every year over the course of a few days, a gathering of wizards, magicians, enchanters, conjurers, and witches from all over the world, takes place.

At the center of it all, the human form of a time exacting machine guided a group of 5 youngsters and me -dressed at times as colorful harlequins (as in court jesters) - on a 24 hour-long journey to become wizard apprentices.

Throughout our quest, we were challenged to learn 3 essential human virtues and 3 perilous vices to avoid. To achieve this: First, we had to find 6 statues possessing them. Second, we were imparted teachings by the statues -each one of them impersonating book antiquarians- followed by our demonstration of the mastery of each virtue and vice. Every time we succeeded, we were granted a clue and a magical power.

The gigantic clock provided us with 2 guides: One called Thumbpee -claiming to be my conscience during our quest. - A spec of a man incessantly showing up, and then suddenly and annoyingly vanishing again and again from my shoulder. The other we named Buggie, a tiny and noisy flying bug that steered us either with the intensity of the buzz from his flapping wings or with a miniature but always timely green laser beam that the nagging bug pointed to lead us in the right direction. Eventually, it was a comforting revelation when we learned from The Orloj that our unruly but very valuable guides turned out to be his sons -the ancient watch's very own long and short hands- acting as our quest's compass.

With each of the clues and powers earned, we were able to overcome a string of non-stop -seemingly impossible- obstacles along Prague's Hradcany Castle's tunnel under the Vltava River. On each hurdle, we had to show our practical knowledge of each one of the virtues or flaws we'd learned. Throughout, our good judgment and common sense under extreme pressure and stress were tested.

Once we reached the other end, The Orloj was waiting for us at the castle's doorstep. Soon after, at the adjacent National Library -called the Klementinum- he rewarded us with our credentials as wizard apprentices. Then he extended an invitation to continue our apprenticeship the following year, on the same dates, same wizards, magicians, enchanters, conjurers, and witches' gathering but at a different and intriguing new location.

In the second book of the series "The Orloj of Venice," the human version of The Orloj inhabited the San Marco Square's astrological clock. The narrative delved into the adventure that took place the following summer. Once again, the six of us were led by the eccentric time measuring device, and accompanied throughout by his sons, Thumbpee and Buggie. One more time, this time through the streets, water channels, and palaces of the fabled and beautiful city on the water, we were challenged to learn 3 valuable attributes, and 3 flaws to be found in any fellow human being. Once we mastered them, we were able to begin the perilous crossing of "the never-ending" bridge over Venice's Bay, once more as attempted to cross it, we were challenged with obstacles that could only be overcome with our knowledge of the 6 human virtues and flaws previously learned, this time our reward when completing the bridge crossing was to become fully accredited young wizards.

Our third Orloj adventure begins in the same place as last year, the institute where I teach...

Erasmus Cromwell-Smith II
Written in T.D.O.K in 2058.

PREFACE

Hells Canyon National Recreational Area
(Summer 2057)

There is not sign of civilization. Just miles and miles of rolling hills and white sandy beaches by the riverside. The cold and crystalline waters are a refreshing contrast to the scorching summer temperatures. Lush greens and yellows paint the gentle slopes that frame both sides of the Snake River.

Professor Erasmus Cromwell-Smith II and his other half, tech savant Lynn Tabernaki, lazily float adrift -face and body up- at 2 to 3 mph over the pristine waters. Their river raft, kayaks in tow, follows them a few hundred yards behind. At the helm, their guide is a high-school professor from Lewistown -a small town that was their expedition starting point.

They soon will be setting camp for the night on a beachhead protected from the stream. Twenty miles navigated for the day is their tally. Tomorrow the adventurous twosome will on their kayaks, spend the whole day as they navigate rapids that will reach category 4 in difficulty.

Under a star-studded sky, lying around a cozy sparking bonfire, Erasmus' upcoming academic year looms largely on Lynn's mind. Her curiosity devours her inside. She's been waiting for a moment like this when his hermetic childhood memories may be probed. Maybe. Just maybe.

"So you'll be taking the whole class to your Orloj adventure in Paris?" she says.

"Not exactly," Erasmus replies.

13

"What's the twist?" Lynn presses.

"That year, the path to the Orloj had a few twists and turns," he replies.

"You mean in other countries?" she asks.

"No, other places in France where precious astrological clocks exist," He responds cryptically.

"You totally lost me," Lynn says.

"That's why you are once more invited to attend the class via web link," Erasmus says.

"You already know I will. I don't understand the big mystery," she says protesting without conviction.

Predictably he doesn't budge. Yet, she tries once more.

"Last year you narrated that when you were 13-years-old your bunch and you went from Wizard Apprentices to Young Wizards. What about the following year?" She asks.

"Master Wizards, Lynn. When the six of us became 14 years old we attempted to become Master Wizards on a quest that took us throughout France," he says in perfunctory fashion.

The "virtually nothing" Erasmus shares is at least a small consolation to her burning curiosity, the rest will have to wait until his course is imparted.

Over the course of the week, Lynn and Erasmus end up rafting 130 miles of the Snake River. Through a totally unspoiled postcard perfect nature reserve. By the time they return back to Lewistown, they are rested and ready to go back to the bay area. Yet the Orloj of Paris is firmly on their minds, a magical journey down memory lane, ready to be uncorked by the eccentric pedagogue.

"Hyperloop Station" (Fall 2057)
California Central Valley's main station

After a short ride from downtown San Francisco's Hyperloop's main station, on an oversized "pill-shaped" cabin, riding inside of a tube; propelled by air-pressure inducting engines, on a near-vacuum state, at a speed close to 500MPH, Professor Erasmus Cromwell Smith II disembarks filled with enthusiasm and expectations. This being his first day of class for the academic year, it is always a special occasion he savors. As the pedagogue unlocks the bike he now has on location at the station's storage room, he reflects on the adventure he had in France 25 years earlier; pedaling with a care-free cadence, he slowly makes progress towards the institute's campus. Ten minutes later in the distance, the glass and steel low-rise buildings come into view.

"The Central Institute of Arts and Literature"
(Fall 2057)

Dressed in pasty yellow corduroy from head to toe, his customary leather backpack on one shoulder, the eccentric professor walks the halls of his faculty with a spring in his stride.

"Walking to class. Already at the institute," he texts Lynn.

"You're late as usual, we're all here waiting for you," Lynn replies.

He smiles at the news that after all his significant other has been able to join through a video-link.

"LOVU," he deflects.

"ME2, you are incorrigible," she replies.

In typical fashion, when Professor Erasmus Cromwell Smith II enters the room, he is late. This time by only five minutes. But nobody seems to care, much less him. He walks towards the auditorium's stage sporting the broadest of smiles. As customary his class is being broadcasted to all the nation dominions. Besides the 500 students in the auditorium, another 14,000 are attending via a live video web link.

"How was your summer?" he asks with a thunderous, energetic tone.

"Insanely awesome Professor!" is the collective response he gets from the student body.

"For the third academic year in a row, we will return to Europe. The summer adventure that took place that year occurred in France. Once again through the beauty of poetry and the wisdom of timeless fables, we will be traveling back in time to an amazing experience I had when I was fourteen years old. As with our previous two classes, first in Prague then in Venice, this is the first time in my life that I am sharing these memorable anecdotes with anyone," he says, sips a bit of water, and continues, "Please refrain from using any of your personal communication devices, this will be my only warning about this subject, if any of you still decides to use them, you'll be doing so at your own peril," he adds.

"Although it did not start that way; Everything in France became more challenging and perilous, yet at the same time amazing and unforgettable," the professor says.

"Join me please then once more on a journey back in time," he says.

"The story begins like this…"

"INTRODUCTION"
(Summer 2032)

*H*owling winds lift countless autumn leaves, sending *them twirling into dawn's nascent lights; Rain's aroma is omnipresent, creek rumbles turn into furious roars. Dust is blown away, pelting everything and blurring it all. Clouds gather quickly; in delayed motion, thunder clashes follow the electric lights show. Dark forces lie in wait for the young wizards. They know the gritty bunch will arrive soon. This time though, the world of the occult will be implacable. It seeks revenge and will not allow being ridiculed once again. The young magician's failure is the only outcome they'll accept. Nature is restless as black magic is in the air. The twisted spirits of those after the young wizards are boiling inside, getting ready for an epic confrontation.*

(The Six Young Wizards)

During the last twelve months, the six of us have become close friends. Although we bonded extremely well during our adventures in Prague and Venice, each experience only lasted for 24 hours. And each of those two days were so intense, we barely had time to get to know each other; yet, during the last twelve months, incessant chats, impromptu video calls and text messages have become a staple in our lives. It has been a fluid and immersing experience as we were already quite comfortable and trusting with one another. In other words, the team spirit and two successful quests under our belts have been the perfect Segway for the camaraderie and strong affinity we have developed for each other since then.

We are a diverse group of six gritty fourteen-year-old young wizards. Our heads are full of questions about our upcoming adventure in Paris. We are also constantly debating when and how we will use our powers throughout the duration of our quest in France. During our first stints in Prague ad Venice, each of us went by a nickname: Sofia Casal aka Reddish comes from Barcelona, Spain. The daughter of the leading pianist and violinist of Barcelona's philharmonic orchestra. Passionate and highly opinionated, she's always challenging and philosophizing every situation. Sang-Chang Lin aka Breezie comes from Shanghai, China. Studious and bookish, he is nevertheless quick to action and an extremely gifted acrobat. Minnie Mubate aka Checkered comes from Pretoria, South Africa. She is a precocious soprano in the famous Praetorian choir. She has an adeptly analytical mind and yet she is extremely perceptive and fiercely loyal. Carol Jamal aka Greenie comes from Beirut, Lebanon. She is a leading character in her country's most popular teenager's TV program. She is vivacious, extremely curious, and impulsive. Above all, she is a great team player. Sanjiv Kalwani aka Firee comes from Bangalore, India. He is a computer and electric gadgets genius. His mind works at warp speed. He is constantly questioning or making the cleverest observations about everything. As for me, Erasmus Cromwell-Smith II aka Blunt, I come from Boston, USA. I am being raised by my adoptive parents, they are both senior citizens. And as they are both retired and travel a lot around the world with me tagging along, they've home-schooled me since an early age. At present we are living temporarily in Wales in the small town of Hay-On-Wye, also known as Book Town, where my father was born and raised. And this suits me just fine as my natural inclination and proclivity in life, are the antique books stores that abound in my current hometown.

(Video conference among the six of us, young wizards)

"Where are we going to meet Blunt?" asks Greenie.

"At the "Gare Du Nord" (train station of northern Paris)," I say.

"Same date and hour?" asks Breezie.

"One day earlier, same agreed time," I reply.

"Why a full day ahead of our scheduled encounter with the Orloj?" Firee asks.

"Guys, it is pretty obvious that this time around, it'll be a lot more challenging to find the ancient clock," opines Reddish.

"That's right, there are a few puzzles we need to solve beforehand," I say.

"Blunt, my parents are still uncomfortable with your Italian aunt and American uncle chaperoning the six of us for two whole days," points out Checkered.

"Well, they are both parents themselves so they'll have no problem keeping an eye on us," I say.

"That's pretty much what they need to be reassured on. Just to meet and chat and get to know them better," Checkered says.

By the nodding heads, I sense that the parents of my other four mates have the same concerns.

"Guys, bring just a small backpack on your shoulders, don't show up with any suitcase, we are going to be on the move all along," I say.

"I am bringing my tablet, that's not a problem right?" asks Firee.

"All of us must take along all the computing fire-power we possess. We may need it, especially in the hours ahead of our quest," I say.

"See you all in Paris then," I say.

"See ya!" is the response in unison of all my mates before we close the video call.

Hay-On Wye, Wales

The greatest surprise of my life occurs when I walk over to my mentor in town. A wizard by the name of Winston Wildenkoss, he is Hay-On-Wye's book antiquarian specializing in the world of magic. On the eve of my train ride to Paris, enthusiastically I march through the town's army of antique books stores, en route to my favorite store in town, "Wildenkoss Antique Books from the World of Magic" (Est. far back in time). But when I turn the corner, his store is no longer there. I cross the cobblestone narrow street and stand in front of a brand new Pub!

'How can this be possible? Mr. Wildenkoss' store was here a couple of days ago,' I mull over.

For a brief moment as I stare at the pub's sign; my wide startled eyes become even more so. The familiar voice comes from nowhere.

"Young Erasmus, my job is done, you no longer need me here, see you in Paris," he says.

(En route from Wales to London)

The early morning "Welsh-Regional" train I boarded in Hay-On-Wye -my place of residence at present- is in desperate need of an upgrade along with an update. It is an inconspicuous, nondescript, insufferably slow means of transportation; only its efficiency and punctuality save the day for "the crawler" as I've just nicknamed it to make its way through all the way to the Victoria Station in London.

Little do I know what awaits me along the way to the British Capital. But more of that further ahead. Hours later, after a puzzling yet amazing ride, I meet my uncle Bart, who has flown in on an overnight flight from Boston, at the train station I am somehow not only relieved to get off the wicked rail car, but in particular, increasingly thrilled to be much closer to Paris, the 2000+ years old city of light.

Victoria Station, London

My favorite person in the world after my parents hugs me long and tight. The bond and affinity that unites us is absolutely natural. Ever since I remember, whenever Bartholomeous Emerson-Lloyd is around, I can freely open-up from my "shell of shyness" while feeling totally at ease, within my comfort zone.

"Look at you, you must have grown 3 to 4 inches during the last 12 months, how tall are you now?" he asks.

" 5' 11" " I say.

"At 14? Erasmus you are going to be a bean pole!" he says.

I stare at my American uncle with admiring eyes that nevertheless denote my utter ignorance about the words he is using.

"Tall; at the growth rate I see, you'll soon be quite a tall lanky youngster," he says with benign eyes filled with his usual warm affection for me.

"We have 90 minutes to spare, let's eat, your extending frame needs lots of nutrients," he says.

We walk towards one of the countless coffee shops within the station. From afar I see her and my face lightens up with a big broad smile.

"Surprise!" My Italian aunt Maria Antonella D'Agostino says standing up and heading towards me with long and effusive strides.

"I did not expect to see you here," I say while we hug and kiss on both cheeks.

She holds my hand and does not let it go as we sit at her table.

"I wouldn't have missed your new adventure for the world," she says.

I smile and nod in slow motion, welcoming back my two trusted guardians and companions.

"Erasmus, this time though, once through with your third encounter with the Orloj, you are coming with me to Milan. My brother, your uncle Roberto has made me promise that I'll bring you over to spend time with your cousins, both mine and his kids. So you get acquainted with our side of the family," she says.

"Deal," I say.

As our Eurostar train bound for Paris quickly gathers speed towards the euro-channel -the underwater crossing to France- I am still reeling about my previous train ride. My facial expression quickly gives me away.

"Something happened on the train ride from Wales," I announce.

"Train ride from Wales to London (2032)"
(A couple of hours earlier)

The regional train is efficient but Spartan in terms of comfort, amenities, and especially the dining experience. But above all is utterly slow by European standards. It moves around seemingly at a snails' pace. My ride is transpiring as it always does, with great views and sightseeing of the Welsh and English countryside. I am surrounded by placid but mute commuters on the way to work in London, for many their stay will last the whole week workdays and they won't be back home until the weekend. Hence today is another normal routinary day, so it seems at first, but I couldn't be more wrong...

It seems initially just a colorful piece of cloth. A glimpse on my part through the panoramic glass window. I glance ever so briefly at what amounts to passing flying colors. My eyes are fixated outside. I am not quite certain of my sighting. Then I see it again. Actually, this time there are many of them. Next, the carousel of colorful cloths forms into a single whirlwind that dives at lightning speed through the window into my train car. Nothing happens for what seems like an eternity, although it is just for an instant. The faint melody catches me by surprise and seizes my attention. It is a tune I am quite familiar with. "The piper is somewhere in the vicinity, and when he is around, good things happen."

I recall from last year's adventure in Venice.

I look around the train car but cannot find a thing. On my second pass scanning the passengers, I noticed her! A tiny old and pale lady. In fact, even if it sounds strange, it is her clothes that catch my attention. In particular, the colors of the flower arrangement on her floppy hat, the unmistakably beautiful and unique color combination that moments ago flew through the window. When I fix my view on her, I realize she is staring at me with benevolent-motherly eyes. Then, unexpectedly, with a small hand gesture, she waves, inviting me to come, then softly pats the place next to her for me to sit. Like under a spell I feel the intense pull and magnetism that seconds later has me walking to her.

"C'mon young man, have a seat," she says.

As I do, the tiny old lady smiles warmly while gently patting the top of my hand. Somehow her gesture makes me feel at ease, even safe. I don't know who she is, not even what she wants, only that purportedly she has just come flying through my window.

"The flower arrangement on my hat always gives away," she says.

'Who is she?" I ponder all by myself. So I think.

"Soon, you'll find out," she says to my great surprise, reading my mind once more.

"Are you a..?" I ask.

"I am many things, depending on the place and circumstances. But in particular who I am with. For you today, as I was for someone very close to you in the past, I'll be a mentor," she says with a crisp and soft voice.

Her words spark a wave of questions and curiosity in me. Yet for no reason I can discern, I say nothing and decide to listen.

"Dear young wizard," she says revealing what I already sense.

'A witch!' I realize in excitement.

With a mischievous smile she pauses, letting me come back to earth, then continues,

"Besides introducing myself, the reason I came to see you here while on your way to London, is to provide assistance on your quest," she says.

My dreamy eyes have a soothing effect on her tone of voice. Progressively it morphs from warm and mentoring to a loving and grandmotherly whisper. Her next set of words do not shock me at first.

"There is no astrological clock in Paris," she says.

"I already know this. It must exist in the -other- Paris, the one populated by wizards and witches," perhaps getting ahead of myself, I reply too quickly.

"In order to gain access to where the Orloj resides, the astrological clock you seek must exist in the real world, that's the only place where you'll find the entrance into the parallel world of the city of light," she says knocking the wind out of my sails.

"Where am I going to find the Orloj in Paris then?" I plead.

"That's why I'm here. C'mon, let's go for a ride," she says.

Suddenly, I am absorbed into a wind twister of colors. I see myself exiting the train through the window into the open air, then leaving the train altogether, accelerating to lightning speed shooting straight-up towards a cloudless blue sky.

The ground below seems distant and yet we are crisscrossing it at a vertiginous speed. Soon I see the English coast; moments later we zoom past it and over the English Channel. Within seconds the French coast is just ahead of us.

The old lady's words resonate in my head. The absence of an astrological clock in the French capital is a problem that has troubled me and my fellow young wizards, all year long. As we enter the continental European coast my new mentor knows what I am thinking.

'In order for you to make it to the right place in Paris where your adventure will begin, you have to get to the Orloj first. In order for this to happen, you'll have to solve the riddle of this location through six different astrological clocks located throughout France,' she thinks for me to hear while we fly, 'I want you to understand, where we are heading, it is of most importance that you remember the locations we are going to visit, they are all essential for you to find the path that will ultimately take you to the Orloj,' she says, 'coming from Wales on a south easterly direction we exited the English coast through Southampton. We have now just entered France through the Normandy Coast, underneath is the French city of Le Havre and slightly ahead is the beautiful medieval town of Enfleur,' are the thoughts she transmits to me.

We make a 45-degree bank to the left and are immediately flying over a sinuous and twisting river, 'that's the famous Seine River that continues all the way to Paris,' are the words she thinks for me to hear as we descend at vertiginous speed into a medium-sized city right by the river's side.

Rouen, Normandy (2032)

We are standing in the middle of an old cobblestone street. I can see a magnificent astrological clock right above us on an arch crossing the road. The street corner sign plaque reads.

"Rue Du Gros-Horloge" (street of the big clock).

"Young wizard, let me introduce you to the Gros-Horloge Du Rouen. It is an extraordinary timepiece both in craftsmanship and complexity. Built in 1329 (14th century). It is the oldest astrological clock in France; through its Renaissance-era facade you can easily note that it was built in the 16th century, 1529 to be precise. It includes a golden sun with 24 rays; a blue background sprinkled with stars and a dial 2.5 meters (7.5 Ft.) in dimension; the oculus on the upper side of the dial shows the phases of the moon over a 24-day rotation. At the bottom of the dial the different days of the week are displayed, each with a different theme," she explains, "It is for you to find out what role this clock plays in finding the Orloj," she adds.

Before I have time to react she is already on the move, "time continues young man."

And just like that, we are back in the air, twisting and turning in a whirlwind of colors, zooming through the sky at the speed of light.

"Eurostar Train"
(En route from London to Paris)

My auntie and uncle look at me with eyes sparkling in bemusement and curiosity.

"Where else did you go with her?" my aunt Maria Antonella asks.

"That's the problem, I don't remember anything else after that first visit. Except the loudspeaker waking me up with the announcement of the arrival of the Welsh regional train to London's Victoria Station where I met you both.

"There has to be something else you remember," says my uncle Bartholomeous.

"All I know is that she said that she was going to take me to six astrological clocks in France. All or some play a role in finding the Orloj in order to start my upcoming adventure, but I still don't know which of them play a role or in what pecking order they should be visited,"

"What about her?" asks my aunt.

"I don't even know who she is!" I reply although an eerie feeling keeps on building inside of me on the subject.

"Gare Du Nord"
(Northern Paris, train station)

The six of us high-five and pile on, hyper excited to see each other in person after one year. In the meantime the parents of my five fellow adventurers are having a round table with my aunt and uncle in one of the station's coffee shops. It seems from afar an animated conversation. I feel bad for them; my aunt and uncle are being peppered with questions by my mates' parents.

"What are we doing next?" Asks Reddish.

"If all of you are good to go, we will be heading first to the city of Lyon," I reply.

"Why Lyon of all places?" asks Breezie.

"We are all clear that there are no astrological clocks in Paris, right?" I ask.

"Confirmed, even my parents helped me to do one more in-depth web search," says Firee.

"There are six remarkable astrological clocks scattered around France," he adds.

"We are starting with the closest to Paris; the one in Lyon," I say.

I narrate to all, the magical occurrence on the train from Wales, including that I do not recall where I was except the amazing magical trip to the Rouen astrological clock. My five fellow young wizards look at me mesmerized.

"Why aren't we going to Rouen first then?" asks Firee.

"The Rouen astrological clock is on an arch over a street, too small in my opinion, we need to figure out the role it plays though. We need to go to the other five first," I say and everyone looks at me with puzzled eyes.

"What are we looking for then?" Breezie asks breaking the spell.

"We don't really know at this moment," says Greenie.

"Maybe a portal to the Orloj," says Checkered and we all nod with half-smiles and our wide eyes sparkling in realization.

"Gare D'Lyon"
(Paris train station to Lyon)

With my aunt and uncle easily winning over the hearts of my five fellow young wizards' parents; they are now officially our chaperones. All of us wave goodbye from the French bullet train's (TGV) massive windows. The five couple's faces express both excitement and trepidation as their precious cherubins depart on a new Orloj adventure.

(En route by train from Paris to Lyon)

"Young wizards, Maria Antonella and I have been entrusted with a great responsibility by your parents. As we take this very seriously, here is what we expect of you..." says my uncle Bartholomeous as he sets rules for us in the next couple of days.

We barely pay any attention to my diligent aunt and uncle. Suddenly, the panoramic window of the galloping train is regaling us with the same colorful flashes I experienced earlier on the train from Wales to London. A twirl of ragged clothes with a unique and unmistakable color combination. It twists and turns as it zooms through the air in every direction, coming and going in fractions of a second.

"She's out there". I say while our doting chaperones, beside their distracted facial expressions, do not seem to have noticed a thing.

"The old wizard lady is tagging along for the ride. She's watching over us," I say in wonder. But inside I have this nascent and bugging eerie feeling.

"Lyon"

We look like a group of students on a summer trip, backpacks on our shoulders, some wearing baseball caps, most wearing sneakers; my aunt and uncle looking like our tour guides, perhaps even our teachers, without any hurry or time pressure, we stroll around the empty pedestrian streets of the beautiful Lyon's city center. Lazily, we head towards the town's fabled astrological clock.

The aromas of the town all come out on the quietness of a cloudless Sunday sky. Freshly baked bread, pastries and freshly brewed coffee, the strong scent of French cheeses and countless regal flowers, even broccoli can be felt at a distance. Then everywhere, there are the street artists and performers, acrobats, jugglers, handcrafters, painters. But especially we see musicians, singers, violinists, piano players. But it is the accordion player who captures our attention. He's blind and reminds all of us about a couple of similar characters we ran into in Prague and Venice. We glance at each other in complicity and Greenie immediately lets her effusiveness out of the window.

"Votre melodie cete tres belle, (your melody is quite beautiful)", she says in flawless French.

"Thank you, you are very kind. Your French is excellent but it wouldn't be polite towards your five friends if you and I only spoke in French, wouldn't it be?" he says with perfect English diction.

"How do you..?" Greenie begins to ask about him picking up that we are a group of six. But she is interrupted by the blind street musician.

"The sound of your steps," he says with a big wide smile that is seconded by Greenie as well.

"Perhaps you could help us," she says.

"It'll be a pleasure. But tell me, what kind of assistance you could be seeking from a handicapped man like me?" the blind street musician says.

"Our encounters with people with your kind of handicap have always rendered great outcomes to the six of us," interjects a matter of fact Breezie.

"I like your bunch's assertiveness. Ok spell it out then," he says with a mischievous smile.

"You already know what we are going to ask you, isn't it right?" Breezie counters.

"Perhaps I do, perhaps I don't. Does it really matter?" he counters.

"We need information about the Lyon astronomical clock," Reddish blurts out not being able to contain herself.

"Predictable...That's a request I've received many times before," he says in a pensive tone along with a satiated expression.

"Let's take a walk," he says shouldering his accordion while leading the way into the street maze ahead of us. He promptly takes us to the cathedral of Lyon. The clock is enormous. As if reading my mind the blind accordion player says...

"The clock is one of the oldest in Europe. It is 27Ft (9 meters) tall. It was built sometime within the 14th century and was destroyed in the 16th century. Subsequently, it was restored in the 17th century and finally in 1954. Unfortunately, it has been inactive since 2013. So, except for the clock's mechanisms, we are going to focus on everything else it has: The astrolabe shows the data and position of the sun, the moon, the earth, and the stars in the sky over Lyon. The sun is depicted circling the earth. The clock's central tower octagon houses multiple automaton figures. They all freeze at the sounding of the horn. Except for a Swiss guard, all other moving figures are religious in nature. The astronomical clock rings every day at noon, 2, 3, and 4PM. Unfortunately, as I said earlier, the clock is not working at present," he explains.

'What are we doing in front of a non-working clock, there has to be an ulterior motive to it,' I reflect trying to stay focused.

We contemplate every little detail of the ancient clock the blind man has just described. We then talk about its history some more with the erudite blind man. I turn and stare with a clueless face at my uncle and aunt. They are sitting across the street in a coffee shop having a good time. Both smile and wave encouraging me to go on. Our gentle guide plays again his accordion giving us all the space in the world to absorb and interpret his words. A nagging thought ever since I met the tiny old lady on the train continues to bug me. As time passes the eerie feeling continues to grow.

'I might just as well find out,' I think.

"Sir, perhaps.." I begin to say but our improvised guide interrupts me.

"Herve, call me Herve," he says.

"Mr. Herve perhaps you can help us enter the mechanisms of the clock," I say.

"Why on earth would you attempt something like that?" he asks.

"To find out if there is anything inside the clock that may help us. Besides, we all six have already been inside the astrological clocks of Prague and Venice and their inner chambers are enormous," I say.

"Such an intrusion will help you with what?" he asks puzzled.

"A noble purpose they can't divulge, can you help them?" interrupts with a broad smile my uncle.

"I don't know," the blind man says while slowly pacing and scratching his head.

"Perhaps you could lead us to the clock keeper?" asks Firee.

"I can see that your bunch is well versed about astrological clocks. Lyon's astrological clock master, who oversees and maintains what is left of it, is a grumpy and very difficult old man. He's been at the job for decades. He never talks to anyone. Let me caution you, there have always been many rumors about him, none of them good. But if you insist, I can certainly introduce him to you. Good luck with that," he says.

"Where can we find him?" Checkered asks.

"That's actually very easy indeed," he replies pointing a finger at a man in overalls going up towards the clock's dial on a motorized scaffold suspended on two cables. We see him tinkering with the clock using his toolbox.

"His name is Salvatore Cacciopo, born in Marseille, of Italian ancestry, he has been the astrological clock's keeper for the last forty years," the blind street musician says as we watch our target descend on the electrically powered scaffold. He is a small man with a pouchy belly and a mane of white unkempt hair.

Mr. Herve approaches the clock master with us tagging along. Before our guide is able to address him, as he reaches the ground level, the angry clock tinkerer, snaps out aggressively, " What do you want blind old man?"

"I have a group of youngsters that want to meet you and ask some questions about the clock," the blind man says with measured words. The nasty man takes a quick glance and quickly dismisses us with a hand gesture.

"Leave me alone, you hear?"

Having said so he turns around and walks away.

My instincts kick into gear, 'We can't lose him,' I realize. Putting a bit of pressure on myself works. I know exactly what to do.

"Temperatore, wait a minute!" (clock keeper in Italian) I say.

He stops right on his heels but doesn't turn.

"Sir, we are supposed to meet an ancient but exacting machine called the Orloj tomorrow in Paris. But at present don't know exactly where! We believe that somehow visiting the clock you oversee is important, as it may help us find clues on how to locate him," I say.

The Temperatore turns around and stares at us with eyes of fire. We all get a hold of each other not knowing what to expect.

"They already succeeded in Prague and Venice," says my aunt from our backs.

"Follow me," he says abruptly.

We all walk in formation behind him inside the clock building. A massive wooden door lies at the end of the ground-level corridor. The Temperatore pulls out a huge black iron ring and selects an even bigger key to open it. The heaviness of the cracking sound that follows creeps through my skin. The narrow wooden stairs that we climb in the narrow tower are poorly lit. The sudden stampede of doves and pigeons above rattles us even more. When we finally reach the clock's wooden mechanisms, the utter sound of the clock bell ringing totally deafens us.

"You've got one hour," he says and I realize for the first time that both the blind man and the Temperatore have been speaking in perfect English all along. Or is it that everything they say we understand in our language.

Once settled in, surrounded by the incessant ticking mechanisms, I ask myself 'isn't the clock not working? what on earth we are expecting to find here?' There's an open area exactly behind the enormous sphere of the clock's dial. We all wander around observing aimlessly. Our surroundings are dusty and predominantly built out of wood. There's natural light filtering from the top of the tower and illuminating the dial from the outside. As I move between shelves filled with tools, inadvertently I kick something on the floor. I glance at it but it has moved further underneath the bottom shelf. I kneel and reach out until

I get a hold of the object. It is a small book! Pulling it out I dust it off and show it to everyone.

"L'magique en l'vie" is the title. It is gorgeous. Its lapis lazuli blue and gold color jump at us. Suddenly inundated with beautiful and unforgettable memories a knot starts to form in my throat. Slowly, everything starts to make sense to me. The growing gut feeling is for a good reason after all. That's when I decide to do a video call with my father. With everyone around me wearing puzzled faces, seconds later I have my loving parents on the virtual screen of my foldable tablet. Retired university professor Erasmus Cromwell-Smith Sr. and next to him, the love of his life, my mom Victoria Emerson-Lloyd, also a retired college professor.

"Junior, son, how are you?" my dad asks.

"Puzzled dad," I reply.

We all can see how my father's perennially absent-mindedness finally settles and he notices the crowd around me staring at him.

"The whole bunch calling, it must be important I presume," he says.

"Dad, ever since I was a child, you talked endlessly about one of your mentors, an antiquarian lady in your hometown in Wales. She specialized in antique books for the young. You told me that she was your biggest cheerleader all the way to your Oxford and subsequent Harvard stints," I say.

"That's right. Victoria Sutton-Leigh, that was her name," he replies.

"You called her Mrs. V. right?" I ask.

"Yes, in order not to confuse her with your mom," he says.

"Do you have any pictures of her around?" I ask.

"Yes, why?" he says intrigued.

"Dad, go and fetch them please," I plead.

He is back rather quickly and fumbling through a thick photo album. He pages through it until he shows us the page pointing to a small picture.

"She was never much into photographs. This is the only one I have of her," he says looking at the small image.

His gesture of disbelief is equal to ours. The picture is blank, there isn't anyone on it.

"Perhaps it has faded over time," he says not totally convinced.

"And all the surroundings are perfect. It doesn't sound right dad. Can you describe her to us please?" I ask as the suspense builds for all listening.

"Everything about her was tiny. Her stature, hands, feet. She had blond hair, very pale, fine features, and blue eyes always hidden behind rimmed reading glasses. Soft voice. Why do you ask?" he says.

"Did she wear a floppy hat with a unique colorful arrangement?" I ask.

"Yes. How do you know this? I don't recall ever telling this to anyone," he says.

"I met her earlier today dad, a sweet, grandmotherly lady that self-appointed herself as my mentor on the spot," I say.

"Son, she died many years ago," my dad says his voice trembling.

"She then flew in through the window of the rail car. She came to help, on this year's quest... As you know Paris does not have an astrological clock so we are going to be visiting France's main astrological clocks, looking for clues that could take us to the portal to the Orloj. Well, she flew me to an astrological clock in Rouen, a small town in Normandy. Supposedly she took me to another five astrological clocks as well but I have no memories of that part of the journey," I say.

My father stares at me intently and says not a word for a long time.

"Son, I can see how convinced you are about this, but Mrs. V. was no witch," he says.

"How do you know dad?" I ask.

"She never did practice or lectured me on any of the sort," he says.

"Dad, have you ever believed in magic?" I ask.

"Actually not. After a magic shop opened in town and I learned all the tricks of the illusionists, I told her that I no longer believed in magic," he says with a lamenting tone.

"Well, perhaps she tried but you never gave her a chance so she mentored you without magic," I say.

My father's eyes widen in realization, "How did you know it was her?" he asks.

"I didn't but had a gut feel, especially once she said to have been the mentor to someone close to me," I say to his fascinated face.

"Dad, there is a precious antique book at home that you and mom read to me since I was a child," I say.

"Of course, that would be 'The Magic in Life'," he says but stops himself short finally getting it.

"Son, is she a..? he asks.

"Yes Dad she is a witch," I reply.

"Dad, can you go and fetch the book please?" I ask him.

Moments later he comes back with the blue and golden book and holds it proudly.

"Can you open it please?" I say.

He does and both mom and his mouths fall open in surprise. We can all see that the pages are empty.

"Dad, Mom we have just found the French version of the same book here in the clock's mechanism's chamber of the Orloj of Lyon," I say showing the book to both of them.

My five young wizard mates are in trance with eyes filled with machinations and possibilities. My aunt Maria Antonella is simply happy enjoying the moment and my own happiness. But it is my uncle Bartholomeous' facial expression that is unforgettable. His hand covering his mouth. His eyes filled with surprise and the memories of that little book that my mom recited to him since he was a little boy.

Now it's my dad's turn. "Son, can you open the book?" he asks.

I do and the gorgeous hand-painted pages jump out immediately. My parents' faces reflect the shock of their lives.

The six of us in turn are delighted to hold what seems to be a valuable clue on our search for the portal to the Orloj.

"Hm, Hm, Hm. Your hour is up," says the Temperatore, breaking the spellbound moment.

We turn and find a much friendlier yet impatient stare on the indecipherable man.

"Temperatore, can we take this book with us?" I ask,

He looks at the book then stares at each one of us for what seems like an eternity. I have zero expectations and kind of expect to be yelled at. But I am in for a surprise.

"That book does not belong to this place, I don't know how it got here," he suddenly says, "As far as I am concerned you can do with it whatever you want," he says with a cryptic tone as if knowing much more that he is letting us see.

(En route by train from Lyon to Besançon)

The book sits wide open in front of the six of us. We page endlessly through it looking for clues. We read aloud and revert to our well-learned -the hard way- practice.

"It's not meant to be understood yet, let's put it aside for the moment," I say.

No soon I've said this, the book cover starts to glow intensely. 'Swipe the cover dear," is the sweet voice we hear in

the background. We turn around looking for Mrs. V but she isn't present. Then I see the twirl of unique colorful cloths flapping outside our window. I point it out to all my mates.

"There she is."

Turning our attention to the glowing book I place the palm of my right hand on top of the cover page. Gently I swipe to the left as if passing a page and the book cover changes!

I swipe it again and a new cover appears. Once six cover pages have been displayed on my seventh try the book cover does not change any longer. I swipe it to the right going backward and every previous cover page comes into view.

"Six books, one for each one of us," says Checkered.

A big question mark is drawn on my face. I slowly turn towards the panoramic view of the bullet train.

"She's gone!" Reddish says as we all stare at the window with incredulous looks.

"How do we split the books?" Asks Greenie.

"I've got an idea. Blunt, when you swipe them, before disappearing, each cover page slides slightly to the side of it," says Breezie when I interrupt him.

"Trying to jump off the book!" I finish his sentence.

Next, I swipe the cover page a bit harder to the right and a translucent glowing book jumps to the side and drops down in slow motion, but when it touches the train cabin table counter's surface, it vanishes with a tiny sparkling puff! I try again and the same thing happens. Our computer genius, Firee suddenly comes ablaze; Without a word he unfolds his tablet, turns it on, and places it next to the magic book.

"Try it again Blunt," he prompts me.

I do and to our amazement this time the glowing book drops inside the tablet, as if absorbed by it.

"Once more," Firee presses. But this time the next book upon contact with the tablet's screen vanishes once more with a minuscule puff!

Firee pauses and stares alternatively at each one of us with intense eyes as he computes what is the right choice.

"Reddish, give me your tablet please," he asks.

He then places her tablet next to the glowing book, " go ahead, Blunt, try it again" he asks.

I swipe it again, this time it works. In the end, each one of us receives one of the six books, and the moment the last one dives into my tablet, the glowing book vanishes altogether. That's when the now-familiar grand-motherly voice of Mrs. V. comes back...

"Very well done young wizards. Now you all go ahead, read and study them. Make sure each one of you goes through all of them. Exchange the books amongst you in the same fashion. Good luck, I'll be around," she says with a tiny wink. Next in a snap, the twirling colorful ragged clothes flapping outside of the window vanish once more.

We are left immersed in our books while my aunt sleeps soundly and my uncle Bart is totally concentrated on the historical book he is reading. We all career at 200mph on the TGV towards the French city of Besançon.

"Besançon"

The six of us contemplate Besançon's Cathedral astronomical clock tower. It has four dials, one on each side of the tower, making the time it marks visible from every angle of the city. Each one of us is struggling with concentrating as we are all still reeling from the lectures the six books are providing.

The distant sound of the flute catches us by surprise. There he is the joyful piper moving along the rooftops with short side-jumps.

'When he shows up good things happen...! ' I remind myself.

"Youngsters, you seem highly interested in the Besançon clock, aren't you?" says a man eccentric-looking sitting on a table nearby.

We glance at him with obvious interest. "A great deal of interest indeed," replies Reddish imitating the regal British accent of the stranger.

The more I look at him; six golden buttons, a double- breasted blue blazer instead of a tie, a scarf around his neck, loafers without socks, a handlebar mustache he keeps on twirling. Once again goose-pimples spread all over me. As we approach him I dial my father and partially covered by my mates' backs, I point the camera to the man's face.

"Where to begin...This is a very peculiar astronomical clock," twirling his mustache, the Brit says, the other hand on chin while carefully observing each one of us. "The clock was built in the middle of the 19th century but was replaced a decade later as the original proved to be faulty, constantly malfunctioning. The clock is almost 6 meters (18ft.) high and 7.5 meters (23 ft.) wide, it contains 30,000+ mechanical parts and 11 movements. In every sense it's a mechanical wonder, its seventy dials provide 122 measurements. Amongst them are the times of eight major cities in the world; from the calendar, it shows; month, date, day; another dial depicts the Zodiac, others the duration of day and night; sunrise and sunset exact times, solar and lunar eclipses, as well as the leap years. A planetarium depicts the positions and orbits of the planets. As the clock was commissioned by the Catholic Church the then Archbishop of Besançon, Cardinal Mathieu, the clock depicts the key dates of the Roman Catholic liturgical calendar; twenty-one automated figures either ring the quarter-hour and the hour or conduct Christ's Resurrection at midday and his internment at 3:00PM. At the top of the clock, a pyramid of figures can be seen; the base consists of the 12 Apostles. Different pairs of Apostles come out to strike each hour. Above, the Archangel Gabriel and Michael strike the quarter-hours moving along with a group of 3 figures underneath, the chalice of charity flanked by the virtues of faith and hope. At the very top of the pyramid and the clock, at noon Christ arises from his grave accompanied by his mother Mary's spirit image. At 3:00PM he goes back to his grave and Mary lowers herself," the stranger says concluding his dissertation.

"Dad, are you there?" I whisper to him while lowering myself trying not to be noticed.

"Junior, yes we are here,"

"Did you recognize him?"

"Who?"

"The man at the table describing the Besançon clock,"

"Son, we thought you had dialed us by mistake, all we've been regaled with all this time while waiting for you to notice your phone is an empty table and your friends and your giggles," my father says.

Lost in my thoughts I do not notice it at first. When I do, it totally embarrasses me.

"Dad, mom, I'll call you guys later," I am caught -in fraganti- phone in hand by all my mates and our generous speaker.

"They can't see or hear me young wizard," the British aristocrat says reading my mind.

I am in total shock but at the same time know who he is.

"Indeed Erasmus, I was your father's mentor as well for many years," he says reading my mind.

"You are Mr. M," I say

"Justin Morris-Rose III, at your service, son,"

"Aka The Equilibrist," I counter.

"Indeed, that's the other moniker your father gave me. Well, I am here to mentor and guide you to the Orloj," he replies.

"Go on then, Sir, the stage is yours," a flustered, like the rest of us, Checkered offers.

"There are many conflicts and disputes within the Besançon clock. None of them exist in the mundane world but in the world of the occult and obscure arts. The most poignant of all arises from the builder of the original clock, Monsieur Bernadine. He built the clock between the years 1858 and 1863. His spirit is still incensed against Monsieur Verite, the creator of the replacement clock between the years 1858 and 1863. In turn, Monsieur Verite's spirit is forever set against Monsieur Goudey for having completely renovated the clock again in 1900. In Verite's angry soul, merely touching the clock created the insult. The Temperatore (the clock keeper) Monsieur Brandibas' spirit holds the key to solve all of these conflicts. He is said to have mastered, while alive, the three virtues showcased in this clock, namely, faith, hope, and charity. Applying them all three, he was able to maintain Monsieur Bernardin, Monsieur Verite and Monsieur Goudey's conflicts at bay until his passing in 1966. Since then it's been an all-out never-ending war between those 3," he says.

"What about the Temperatore's spirit?" Asks the eternally curious Greenie.

" Monsieur Brandibas' spirit is nowhere to be found," says Mr. M aka The Equilibrist.

"How does all of this relate to our search for the portal of the Orloj?" asks a matter-of-fact Checkered.

"That's for you to find out, now if you'll excuse me, Mademoiselle.,"

Morris says as he gently fades away.

We are all left with countless questions unanswered, knowing well -more like hoping- that all in due time will make sense. We shrug our shoulders. Then we realize that my aunt and uncle are standing directly in front of us.

"We shall presume you were talking to someone?" asks my uncle Bart.

"Yes we were, didn't you see..?" I begin to reply but interrupt myself in realization.

"No, actually what we saw was the six of you standing in front of an empty table, you all seemed engaged with someone, we then saw some of you talking to the same empty table!" my aunt says.

We laugh and giggle sharing everything with our dependable protectors. We then all walk carefree back towards the train station. Next, we are off to Strasbourg in the Alsace. A beautiful region north of here, located along the French border with Germany.

(En route by train from Besançon to Strasbourg)

"Dad, we just met Mr. Morris, aka Mr. M., your former mentor," I say.

"I gather that telling you that he's been dead for decades is pointless," my dad says.

With my mates gathered around me, I smile and nod my head.

"Is he then a wizard as well?" he asks with a dubitative tone of voice.

"He absolutely and utterly is, Dad," I reply with a tone of voice filled with enthusiasm.

"This is all shell-shocking to me son, I never imagined..." he says until I cut him off.

"You never believed in wizards or magic Dad. But it seems that though not aware, as we all revert to reading our books as besides deciphering the clues they contain, now we have a new mystery to solve with the astrological clock of Besançon."

It all happens in an instant, this time the twirl of colorful ragged clothes zooms past our panoramic window only a couple of times. On this occasion, we see when it jumps through the window into our cabin. There she is, standing right in front of our table.

"Well, well, well; hello young wizards! I was having a bit of difficulty finding your train. But here we are, how are you all doing on this wonderful day?" says Mrs. V.

Now used to it, I smile while my mates' mouths fall open in slow motion. I glance over and see both my aunt and uncle having a nap. 'They have no clue,' I realize.

"Nice to meet you all, earlier I had the pleasure to meet dear Erasmus Jr. aka Blunt," the tiny lady says, "I gather you all have had the chance to read the books?" she asks.

"We all have started to review them but only have gotten an overview because of the frequent stops," I reply.

"Very well! It is comforting to know you all have realized that you don't have enough time for them all, yet I highly recommend you to at least get the gist of their content. It will be of utmost importance to you in your quest. Now, let me narrow your search and give you a couple of the subjects contained in the books. You should place special emphasis and focus on faith, hope, and gratitude," she adds.

"Now, let me ask you a few questions," she continues. "Reddish who have you guys run into several times on your quests?" Mrs. V. asks.

"The book antiquarians," she replies.

"Right on. Who else Greenie?" Mrs. V. presses.

"The spec of a man, Thumbpee and the annoying utilitarian flying insect, Buggie," she replies.

"Once more accurate, what else is missing. Checkered?" the tiny old lady continues.

"Obviously the Orloj," she replies.

"Not yet complete. Would you help us, Breezie?" Mrs. V. asks.

"The flutist," he replies.

"Excellent. Firee care to contribute?" We are still short," the old antiquarian wizard presses on. "The hideous dwarf!" he blurts out.

"Blunt, anything else to add?" Mrs. V asks turning to me.

I think about it for a little bit. But I am posturing. A smile starts to form on my face. I know it.

"Blind people. Three times to be precise. An old lady in Prague as an avatar for book antiquarian Morpheous Rubicom; an old man that served me as a guide at San Marco Square in Venice ended up being an avatar for book antiquarian Zbynek Kraus and the last one a grumpy accordion player that helped us gain access to the tower and mechanisms of the Lyon astrological clock," I reply letting it all out in a torrent of words.

"Precious young wizards, all of you have become such indeed," Mrs. V. says while reflecting aloud.

"Mrs. V, what is the meaning of this big gigantic question of yours?" asks Reddish full of candid exuberance.

"Dear, that's for each one of you to find out," then while still smiling with grand-motherly eyes, she slowly fades away right in front of our eyes and the colorful swirl of ragged clothes. She then rocketed out through the very same train window she came in.

We are still reeling about our conversation with Mrs. V. when the inquisitive eyes of my aunt Maria Antonella and my uncle Bartholomeous bring us back to reality.

"First you talk to an empty table on the streets of Besançon and now you repeat the same feat, this time to an empty train cabin counter," says uncle rousing us with a teasing smile, "C'mon spell it out guys," he says prompting us in a playful tone. We then proceed to describe everything but before we have time to analyze the riddles in front of us, the train slows down and the arrival to Strasbourg is announced over the loudspeaker.

"Strasbourg"

"This is a fairy tale kind of city," says Reddish as we walk the impeccable streets of the regal city. Every building seems like a small palace. The overall architecture reflects several other eras. It feels timeless. The abundance of flowers in the balconies of the mostly low-rise buildings is not only postcard-perfect but warm and welcoming. Walking through the historical city center called the Grand Ile (Grand Island) we soon see one of its key landmarks; contemplating its ancient time machine, the eight of us stand in front of the magnificent Notre-Dame of Strasbourg Cathedral.

When we hear the words: "Astronomical clock," we join a group of Japanese tourists just with the purpose of listening to the description their tour guide is about to give. "The Strasbourg astronomical clock was built in the middle of the 19th century by

Monsieur Schwilgue. Its first version was probably gigantic in size, 18 meters tall by 7.7 meters wide, to judge by the dimensions of the space it occupied. Its mechanisms were - state of the art- when it was built. The gold hands of the clock measure solar mean time; the silver hands indicate central European time. During winter the solar timer is approximately 30 1/2 minutes behind European central time. Among its different dials and displays are the ornery (planetary dial). A display of the real position of the sun and the moon, as well as solar and lunar eclipses. Built in the clock is the computus which more than likely is the first perpetual mechanical Gregorian calendar ever built. The highlight of the clock though is the procession of the 18" high figures of Christ and the 12 Apostles. This occurs every day at solar noon when a rooster cackles three times.."

Our concentration is broken when a very rude man shoves a couple of us to the sides and walks right through the middle of us, "Get out of my way, the city streets are not only yours," he says.

He walks aided by a cane with a pronounced swing of the hips. The more I focus on his peculiar moves the thought crosses my mind more and more, "Mr. Newton-Payne?" I yell guessing and not sure.

The angry man stops right on his heels, turns around, and looks at us with stern and severe eyes.

"Follow me, young wizards!" he says marching forward without stopping or turning.

"He is the third member of the trio of mentors, all of them antiquarians, my father had growing up in Wales," I explain.

"My mates, my father called him Mr. N. He is a war hero from world war II," I say.

Mr. N. enters a beautiful establishment. We promptly follow. The sign at the entrance reads:

"Strasbourg Museum for The Decorative Arts"

"Young wizards, first of all, yes I am Mr. N. and I was Erasmus Jr's. dad's mentor for many years. My mission today is to help you better understand this city clock. So let's get started, shall we?" he says and we all sheepishly nod. "The Strasbourg astronomical clock has been rebuilt three times. In order to appreciate the true dimension of this clock and find the clues it may contain, you have to be introduced to its two earlier versions," he explains as we approach the exhibit of a golden rooster, "Let's take a look at some of these two versions key elements. On the first version of the clock, this gilded cockerel - still preserved today- is perhaps the oldest preserved automaton in the world. Crafted in the middle of the 14th century, it was made out of copper, iron, and wood; at midday, it flaps its wings and spread out its feathers. The bird symbolizes Christ's passion," my father's old mentor continues, "the second version of the Strasbourg astronomical clock was an extraordinary timepiece, not only for its sophistication as an astronomical measuring instrument but also because of the beauty and richness of its ornaments and decorations. Here you can see the calendar dial, the astrolabe, as well as indicators of eclipses and planets. It contained statues that moved, automated figures, and a six-tune carillon. Here you have a celestial globe that was connected to the clock's movement. Among the many paintings on its panels, there was one that depicted the three fates among other sacred themes. The second version also contained the golden rooster at the top of the clock's cupola," he explains.

"Young wizards, my mission is over, it is now up to you to figure out what if anything in the story of this magnificent clock can help you," he concludes and immediately vanishes in a cloud of tiny stars and lightning bolts.

This time our loving chaperones do not bother asking as

walking alongside they already figured out that we were talking to someone. This time to avoid explaining it twice, I call my parents and soon have the four adults as an audience for us six. Between all of us, we explain everything that just happened in detail.

"Mr. Newton-Payne was always very formal and distant but a dependable mentor and a great man. Junior if I only knew the world that lurked just behind my three book antiquarian tutors," he says, "You only needed to believe in magic Dad," I say in perfunctory fashion.

(En route by train from Strasbourg to Beauvais)

"Guys, we have to use the same technique Mrs. V. used with us," Reddish says.

"Which is?" asks a puzzled Greenie.

"What are the common links between all the clocks?" asks Reddish.

"Isn't it a bit too early to do this exercise?" asks Breezie out of the blue.

"Why?" asks Greenie sounding totally clueless.

"Shouldn't we wait until we visit the last clock?" continues Breezie.

"Not really, I think I have an idea about the solution to what we are looking for," says Firee. "Using Mrs. V's technique, let's highlight our findings," says Firee.

"Greenie?"

"Besides the people we have run into multiple times, like the blind man."

"Reddish?"

"We have to read about the three fates depicted on the Strasbourg clock."

"Checkered?"

"What is the meaning of the Lyon astronomical clock not

working and what is the connection of the six books we found including 'The Magic in Life' with the portal to the Orloj?"

"Blunt?"

"I could add that we have to find the spirit of the deceased Temperatore of the Besançon's clock, Mr. Brandibas, as he holds the key to solving the conflict between the clockmakers of the different versions of the clock. But doing so would be a waste of time, isn't that right Firee?" I say smiling at him.

We stare at each other in complicity, we both know.

"Blunt is right. All our findings are essential for our quest when it does begin. We've been driven to finding and understanding these six clocks in detail for reasons that will come into play later. They will certainly be part of the roadmap but only after we meet the Orloj," he says, "Blunt, finish it off please," he adds, "Guys, we've had the key to the portal from the beginning. Even as Mrs. V. tried to orientate us to it. My final answer to her big question was that we had run into blind men three times, then I realized later on that besides my dad's three mentors: Mrs. V., Mr. M. and Mr. N, the only person other than them that read our thoughts was the blind man, no other than Mr. Kraus. The blind man is Mr. Kraus. We are not looking for a portal. We have to find him. As he has always done with each one of us, he is the one who will lead us into the portal to the Orloj," I say with Firee nodding and as we approach the Beauvais main train station.

"Beauvais"

Spirited, the six of us walk through the streets of Beauvais with our two doting chaperones in tow. The town's cathedral looms over the city but the moment we see the giant astronomical clock, we realize what the town's true wonder is. In utter amazement, we all approach the magnificent clock.

"What kind of tourists are you? A pack of six youngsters with their...Let me guess teachers?" says a short hunched man with rimmed glasses.

"We are visiting and studying astrological clocks around France," says Checkered.

"Ah...interesting," he says pensively. "Anyone that appreciates our town's ancient time exacting machine deserves my total respect. Tell me youngsters, what do you want to know about it," he says now wearing a benevolent smile across his well-weathered face.

"Everything Monsieur, please tell us all you know about it," asks Greenie.

"It'll be a pleasure then. Built by Monsieur Verite in the middle of the 19th century, after he'd built a smaller version in Besançon. It is a 36 ft. high by 18 ft. wide machine. It has 52 dials indicating among other things, the sun and moon's rise and set, the planets' position, the time in 18 world cities, the tides times, and the golden number used to calculate the date of Easter. The large central dial -face- displays Jesus Christ and the 12 Apostles," the old man explains.

"Merci Beaucoup, Monsieur," says Greenie in her perfectly modulated French.

Tipping his black beret, the hunched man leaves us with cautious strides. The cane he uses immediately catches my attention.

"He's blind!" I say as we run after him.

"Mr. Kraus, " I yell but he has already vanished in the crowd.

"Now he knows that we know," I say satisfied.

"Blunt, he won't be available until we have studied and learned from all the six clocks," Checkered observes.

(By train from Beauvais to Ploermel)
This time we all fall soundly asleep and are only awaken by the announcement of the arrival to Ploermel.

"Ploermel"

A short while later the eight of us stand in front of a kiosk in the internal patio of a cloistered building. A stocky man in peculiar religious clothes that seem like a big bathrobe approaches us with a friendly and gentle face.

"How can I help you all?" he asks.

"Perhaps you could, are you some sort of tour guide?" asks Reddish candidly.

"Sort of, at times but day to day I am a brother, part of the motherhouse of the brothers of Ploermel, a catholic organization," he explains.

His words and demeanor make all of us feel at ease.

"What can you tell us about the astronomical clock of Ploermel that lies in front of us?" presses Reddish.

"With pleasure. Built in the middle of the 19th century by brother Bernardin Morin, it was initially mounted inside the monastic building of our congregation. It has ten dials displaying: solar time, calendar, the moon's positions, the months & seasons of the year, the signs of the zodiac, the equation of time (difference between mean and real-time), and standard time to the nearest minute for the whole world, the position of the moon, earth and sun. The view of heavens above Ploermel, the position of the sun on the elliptical, and the centuries. The small black hand you can see rotates every 1000 years. The ornery displays the Sun, Mercury, Venus, Earth, Mars, Jupiter, Saturn, and Uranus; together with the moon, the four satellites of Jupiter, and the six satellites of Saturn. As it was built around the discovery of Neptune, and before Pluto was discovered, neither of these planets is shown," he explains.

"Thank you very much, Sir," I say impatiently.

The brother smiles, bows his head, and walks away with an aura of peace and calmness. Instinctively I turn to my aunt and uncle and they are sporting their usual clueless faces. Then it dawns on me.

'In Strasbourg, they could hear the Japanese tour guide but not this..." I think in realization but interrupt myself as I don't want to lose him this time. I call out the brother, "Mr. Kraus?" he pauses for a moment then turns around morphing into the old trusted antiquarian.

"Congratulations, young wizards, you have all completed your preparation for the quest ahead of you. No magic was involved but only your imagination, studiousness, and attention to detail. Now, if you would, please follow me," he says and we do so in tandem. I notice that my aunt and uncle can now see and recognize Mr. Kraus. We walk out of the cloister and into the city streets. Kraus turns right into a small dead-end cobblestone street. right in front of us once again is his antique bookstore. The sign reads: "Zbynek Kraus. Antique Books for the Dark Arts and Occult Sciences,"

Once inside, comfortably seated in the magic place, we are eager to ask him many questions.

"Why weren't you disguised as a blind man this time?" Greenie asks.

"What about you telling me Greenie, why?" he counters.

"I don't know..." she begins to answer but suddenly, her eyes burst with intensity, "perhaps because we already knew you were doing so or even more importantly, we now can see," she blurts out.

Kraus nods with obvious satisfaction. "Fantastic Greenie, just fantastic! That is right. Your minds can now see clearly what's ahead of you. Further, you'll require all you've learned or noticed in your quest," he adds.

"Finally, before you go, let me read something to you that will also be absolutely necessary on your quest," he says as he walks down the aisle to retrieve the book. Pushing aside several books, he deposits it carefully on an old table. Then after opening it with a marker on the right page, and stars o read to us with gusto.

"Not Everything We Hear is What Appears to Be"
Falsehoods can be deceiving,
and although they reside on the other side of reality's spectrum,
truisms can be elusive as well.
Often we don't mean what we say,
this occurs when what we really think or do
is not in sync with what comes out of our mouths.
When in private we deviate from what we really want
 not only are we not pursuing the truth,
we are also attempting to create a false reality
where we may end up believing our own lies.
Hence detecting false negatives or false positives becomes
an existential imperative.
What we hear,
What is said,
Suddenly loses weight, value, and respect.
What matters then is
what was really meant with words we heard
as not everything we hear is what appears to be,
but something else.

Even if at present, we don't understand it all. We are all too cognoscenti about the importance of the message Mr. Kraus is conveying to us; to ignore it. Experience tells us that it'll become indispensable throughout our upcoming quest.

Chapter 1

"MEETING THE ANCIENT TRUSTED CLOCK ONCE MORE"

Without a single additional word by Mr. Kraus, the familiar filling quickly engulf us. Everything around becomes fuzzy. From afar we can see the blurry images of Kraus, my aunt, and my uncle conducting an animated conversation. Soon we've lost contact with their images and find ourselves inside an enormous chamber made entirely out of wood. The six of us stand on a narrow gangway suspended by cables. Underneath, around, and above us are the mechanisms of a giant clock. The clicking sounds are deafening. In front is the back of a gargantuan translucent dial. The intense white light that reflects on it, shows the shadows of the Roman numerals marking the time of the day as well as the short and long hands working the minutes and the hours. Following the narrow path, tentatively, we walk towards the back of the mammoth dial. There they are the small doors behind the roman numerals of the dial. We are standing on the back of the three o'clock Roman numeral. Our daring mate Greenie takes a step forward and pushes the tiny square door. The six of us peek outside from different parts of the opening. It is nighttime. We are at a height of approximately 3 stories looking down but there is no scaffold this time. Incredulous we look at each other and to our surprise, we continue to be dressed in our street clothes.

"No Harlequin dresses this time around. Perhaps no more?" asks Greenie.

"We'll soon find out," replies Firee observing it all in great detail.

"Guys, let's get moving," I say.

Breezie reacts faster than the rest of us. He places a hand outside and corroborates its stickiness at once, like a spider he moves across the walls of what appears to be a cathedral. We are all soon doing the same climbing down at a rapid pace.

'Guys, do you realize where we are?' asks Firee through a thought.

His words are met with silence as we all start to recognize our surroundings. By the time his next exacting remark comes, his observation does not surprise us.

'This is the freaking Notre-Dame Cathedral, we are in Paris you all,' he reflects, his words filled with wonder and youthful enthusiasm.

We reach the ground level filled with excitement. Looking up to the magnificent structure only increases the emotions running through us. The illuminated majestic city is all around us.

"There is not supposed to be an astrological clock in the cathedral," observes Reddish.

"You mean in the normal everyday Paris but not necessarily in its alternate-parallel reality version," says Checkered.

As we all stare at the gigantic clock, Firee's encyclopedic mind is at work again, "In the mundane reality version of Notre-Dame, there is a massive stained-glass circumferential window. It is adorned with colorful flowers carved on the crystal panes. All of a sudden the thunderous voice catches all by surprise.

"Welcome to Paris young wizards!"

We all turn around to the massive translucent astronomical clock marking the official commencement of our Paris quest.

"This is the third year you've been invited to the annual and largest gathering and festivities of wizards, conjurers, enchanters, and witches from around the world that takes place in several cities around the world. I am sure you all have noticed the differences, especially your circumstances" he says pausing to emphasize our awareness of the facts. "And they are and will be significantly more challenging as you are seeking to become master wizards. Your trek over here to this alternate-parallel version of Paris to meet me has been demanding and intricate. It required the usage of the wisdom and common sense you've acquired and learned so far, and I can proudly say that you've excelled at it," the exacting time machine continues while holding our undivided attention, "Accordingly my traditional discourse will be very brief this year, comparatively speaking to our previous two occasions," he adds, "You're are now fully accredited young wizards, hence require no hand-holding," he says, "Young wizards, this year my advice, guidance, warnings, and clues are all contained within the knowledge and experience you accumulated while visiting the six astrological clocks across France. It is up to you to discern them all. This year you'll be on the lookout for your six antique book mentors without your harlequin clothes, you don't need to be singled out with a special protective status. In other words, no more crutches, youngsters. Once again your six trusted mentors will be hard to find. They'll shape-shift into street vendors, musicians, beggars among others, but their preferred occupation will continue to be that of book antiquarians. As they do every year, their bookstores travel with them. Once you are able to find each one of them, they'll sit with you all to study either a human virtue or a flaw. This year you'll be studying the virtues of respect, tolerance, and selflessness and the flaws of indifference, arrogance, and deafness. Once you've demonstrated to each mentor that you've learned enough of each virtue or flaw, you will be able to move onto the new search for another mentor. But this year though, you will only earn powers when you demonstrate excellence and mastery on your replies when your book antiquarian probes you. Also on this year's quest, you can come and meet me any time you deem it necessary. Your challenge is to ensure that it's meaningful and relevant to your quest, otherwise, you'll be bluntly rebuked by yours truly. Needless to say that in the next 24 hours you'll be up against seemingly insurmountable at-time challenges. Rest assured that each one of you soon enough will find out if you are made out and up to the intricate task of being a master wizard. Once you've found each one of your mentors and they've deemed that you've mastered each virtue and flaw, the Eiffel Tower awaits you. As you climb it, you'll face six challenges that will test how well you've learned each virtue and flaw. If you make it to the top, you'll become a master wizard. Finally, as usual, my two sons, the hands of the clock, will be accompanying you all the way. Thumbpee and Buggie as you so dearly call them will be playing a different role though. Notice please that I've just used a term different than guidance. Let's say that they'll be reactive to your requests more than proactive in anticipating your needs. So, it'll depend entirely on you how useful they are. Ask them whatever you need. With them you'll have an advantage you won't have with me. You can be trivial and goofy on your inquiries but then again, it'll depend on you how useful they are. One more thing, your tablets will work for web searches only. No email, text, or phone will work. Young wizards your 24 hours begin now!" The Orloj says before going into hibernation.

Chapter 2

"WANDERING AROUND AND ABOUT THE CITY OF LIGHT"

Once again the place seems empty without the presence of the ancient exacting time machine.

"Where to begin?" philosophizes Reddish.

"Why don't we ask our -should I say- companions?" proposes Checkered aloud with a sarcastic tone.

"Thumpbee could you be so kind and make yourself present?' I please mocking pompously the situation.

In an instant the diminutive man of pasty white skin sits as usual on my shoulder, one leg crossed, hand on his chin as usual. I have to contort and twist just to have a glance at him.

He has a gesture of utter disdain and is not even looking at me.

"And you Buggie may as well show up if you would, please," says Greenie with a loving voice.

In the blink of an eye, the unmistakable and annoying buzz of the flying bug flapping its tiny wings makes itself present once more.

"So the two of you are like Genies now. We have to call you first then formulate our wishes?" Says Breezie in burlesque fashion.

Neither of our two companions is pleased with their new roles. Thumpbee now reflects contempt in his facial expression. Buggie's buzz on the other hand comes and goes in rapid-fire angry and annoyingly noisy bursts.

"Where should we begin?" I ask both of them.

Buggie's buzz now has a cadence as if he doesn't have a clue. Thumbpee on the other side seems pensive, even mischievous while he stares intensely at us, thinking about our question.

"What do the six astrological clocks have in common?" he says referring to our recent train tour.

I realize that this is the next level the Orloj spoke about. We will be helped and assisted but we have to resolve the issues by ourselves.

"The obvious answer would be that they are all ancient astrological clocks," says Greenie.

"Greenie, we are not looking for an obvious answer," says Reddish.

"What about landmarks?" asks Firee, "Aren't they all landmarks?" he presses.

Thumbpee is all of a sudden gone. Buggie on the other hand flies higher and higher until he is level with the cathedral's highly pitched roof.

"He wants us to follow him upstairs," says Checkered.

We all climb the walls of the magnificent structure. Once we are at eye level with Buggie we see his tiny green laser beam projected across the Seine River.

"Greenie, Firee you are the city experts," I say for them to fill in the blanks.

"That's the general direction towards the Jardin des Tuileries," says Greenie.

"And of the...Louvre Museum," she says pausing as the realization hits us all at once.

Without a word, we descend the walls of the cathedral and head towards the most famous museum in the world. But not soon we take a few steps, we hit a wall we can't see. We try to walk in different directions but are not able to.

"It is transparent," observes Firee.

Yet when he walks towards the cathedral we face no such

obstacle. That's how we find ourselves inside the place of worship. Something is not right though.

"Why did we just simply retreat?" I ask.

"Did we? We couldn't move forward, Blunt," says Breezie.

"I don't think so," I say while I walk back outside with the other five following in tandem. I head in the direction pointed by Buggie until I hit the invisible wall. Using my sticky extremities I start to climb the transparent wall. It proves to be much higher than I thought, thirty or so feet high. My initial assumption also turns out to be wrong, there is a ceiling. But that doesn't deter me; with my back to the floor, clinging from my four extremities -like a bat- I now move through the non-visible ceiling, with every step and hand movement, I try to press and feel the surface trying to find an exit. To my delight, on the next move, my right hand does not encounter any resistance. Next, I go through the opening but not before waving at my mates to follow suit. My last sight of them corroborates they've seen me. Peeking outside I am regaled with a magnificent view of the city. But that's about the only normal thing I can see. The sky is filled with flying shadows and silhouettes of all sizes, some are even riding broomsticks. A couple zoom by, too close for comfort. Then there are countless and incessant flashes, small lightning bolts, and explosions that sound less like a detonation or a thud and more like puffs! They are followed by stardust clouds. Bright fluorescent color rays and vectors point to the sky, they move non-stop and seem to originate from every corner of the city skyline; the noises are deafening, the swooshes inundate the sound spectrum. In the distance, music can be heard on all cardinal points. Even more faintly, laughter and people yelling at each other are still discernible rumblings. With my five mates now next to me, we contemplate the parallel Paris mayhem with trepidation. The yearly festivities of wizards from around the world are clearly in full swing right in front of us.

"The ceiling's opening was the real entry point to the other-Paris," points out Checkered.

Still on the premises of Notre-Dame Cathedral, we walk over the invisible roof until we find the edge. We then descend, with the help of our sticky fingers, through the transparent structure walls, until we are finally standing firmly on the ground of the site of our quest. So we believe at first.

Greenie leads the way, enthusiastically she explains that Notre-Dame sits on a small island in the middle of the Seine River.

"Île de la Cité" (The City Island) it's called. We stroll over a small bridge heading out of the island. That's when we hear thunder in the distance, what happens next is totally unexpected. Unbeknownst to us a high-electrical energy charge, first surges then careens down through the skies at the speed of light towards us. We are caught by surprise by the powerful lightning bolt as it impacts the ground right next to us. The sudden explosion blows us off the ground ever so briefly propelling us hard backwards onto the floor, where we all land. We lie on the ground with a few bruises and scratches but are otherwise unscathed.

"Where do you think you are going young wizards?" is the cranky voice we hear.

Too rattled and stunned none of us answers or moves. Our eyes dart in every direction looking for the voice source but can't find it.

The slight breeze slowly dissipates the cloud of smoke and an acrid smell of the explosion.

In front of us against the bridge rail, there is a small tribune with four stunned-looking figures seated as if they were a jury.

There are three ladies and a man all dressed in black robes wearing cone floppy hats. Their broomsticks lie next to them.

"This year's crop is seemingly one of the worst ever," says with a strident voice one of the strange figures.

"The little ones are so afraid that they can't talk," mocks one more of the intriguing characters.

"Perhaps we should pack and leave. I say we fail them, any of you care for voice vote?" seemingly ready the fourth figure asks the others.

Not understanding quite well yet what's going on, we still don't know how to react.

"Look at them. Afraid and mute and they haven't even started this year's quest. I agree let's vote. Who's in agreement to fail them and leave?

"Wait!.." I blurt out.

The group of four goes silent.

"Who are you?" I ask.

"Do I hear a voice. Did any of you hear something?" mocks one of the nasty witches.

"Come on, mama's boy, speak up!" says another of the wicked ladies with a familiar tone of voice.

"Who are you?" I ask again with a firmer voice.

"We are an impaneled jury," she says.

"A jury? A jury for what?" asks Breezie.

"We have been designated to evaluate whether you are up to the task?" one particularly hideous witch says.

"But..." Reddish starts to complain but she is interrupted.

"No buts or ifs, let's get started," the sole wicked male juror forcefully says.

"Why are you headed towards the Louvre first?" He asks.

"Because Buggie pointed us into that direction?" answers Checkered.

"And you didn't care to ask yourselves whether the flying bug was right or not?"

"Buggie is never wrong," Greenie snaps back.

"What about if you are wrong and his intended target was beyond -further ahead or in the vicinity- of The Louvre?" the nasty wizard presses on.

Doubts quickly creep into our minds. Then I see it.

"Our first destination is The Louvre alright because that's where Buggie's laser ended," I counter to my mates' delight and agreement.

None of the impromptu jurors utters a word.

"You've all made perhaps a more serious mistake at the beginning of this year's quest," says the witch with the familiar voice.

Yeah, I remember her mocking me on the streets of Prague and Venice. She was dressed like a medieval tavern waitress. She seems to know what I am thinking as she continues.

"How do you all know that the way into the parallel Paris is through the invisible wall latch on the ceiling? After all, the Orloj met you before you entered the city through the door in the ceiling of the transparent wall, what about if you were already inside the parallel version of Paris when with the Orloj and the wall was simply there to force you to go into the city through, per example, the church? Otherwise, what does it mean, that the Orloj sits outside the parallel city?" the skeptical witch disserts.

We all look at each other with faces denoting confusion.

This is until we see clarity in Firee's eyes.

"This time around, the Orloj is not in the -other- Paris because in mundane reality there isn't an astrological clock mounted on the walls of Notre-Dame, so he lies in a world of his own isolated by the invisible wall and in between the parallel and real cities of Paris. So we did the right thing to look for an entrance into the other Paris. Besides, we met our guides, or according to the Orloj, this time they are only our companions, Buggie and Thumbpee at the roof of the cathedral seeking the advice and they gave it to us. So we are in the right place and on track," he discerns with brilliant logic. We all nod our consent beaming at him with eyes of pride.

"Besides, the fact that we've run into you means as well not only that we are in the other Paris but also that our quest is occurring as we speak because you are the first obstacle we face," adds Checkered with analytical precision.

Our four street jurors look at us with disdain. Next, in slow motion, they look at each other. Then sighing with resignation, they all vanish in a fraction of a second.

In the background, we can hear their laughter fading as they leave us.

"Sometimes people do not mean what they say," I recall aloud Mr. Kraus' earlier reading.

"Shall we?" invites elegantly Greenie for us to continue.

Exiting the small bridge over the Seine River we are off the "Île de la Cité" (The City Island) that is blended with the city landscape and architecture in such a way that it is hard to distinguish one from the other. We walk alongside the riverbanks and quickly approach a much wider bridge on our left side. The small commotion immediately captures our imagination. There is a small crowd on one of the sides of the bridge. Curious, we deviate from our intended path and enter the bridge. There is a rather short yet muscular man standing on the rails of the bridge. His piercing blue eyes stand out. His mane of unruly hair is parted in the middle. He is wrapped in chains and his arms are tightly secured in the back. I count three boxy hand-cuffs in all locking his hands. His legs are also shackled. We realize quickly that everyone around are spectators and the voluntary act is a show.

"What's the point for a wizard to put up a spectacle for an act he can accomplish with a snap of the fingers?" asks a skeptical Reddish.

"Do you really think it would be that obvious?" Asks

Thumbpee all of a sudden sitting once more on my shoulder, "Begin by asking yourself, who is the man about to jump?" The diminutive man asks before vanishing once more.

At that point, the stunt man jumps. It catches us by surprise. Checkered gasps. Greenie grips my forearm. Reddish covers her mouth. In the brief instant he is in the air, the acrobatic man is already contorting furiously to free himself. As he hits the water it seems as if he is already well on his way to free himself up. Within a minute of being submerged, he is back on the surface, while all of us in the crowd cheer loudly for him. Then, as he swims to the riverbank along with a few of the spectators, we exit the bridge and head in his direction. When he pulls himself out of the water, our living encyclopedia is ready for him.

"I know who you are," says Firee.

The man looks at our mate with contempt.

"Everyone knows who I am," the wet performer says.

Then a glimmer of recognition crosses his eyes.

"Ah! A young wizard I gather. The new crop, you may be forgiven then. So tell me how you know about me. I haven't been around the mundane world in more than a hundred years, the acrobat says now wrapped in a towel.

"You are the greatest illusionist and escape artist that ever lived. You are the great Harry Houdini," Firee says with a huge smile on his face.

"A compliment coming from someone that came to the world almost a century after my natural death is something I appreciate very much," he says.

We all now in some fashion form or another have realized who the great little man is. Predictably Greenie's natural curiosity takes over.

"So, Mr. Houdini you are a master wizard after all," she says.

"What is the point behind your rhetorical assertion young lady?" he asks.

"The escape you've just performed did not involve magic," Reddish continues unfazed.

"Of that, you can rest assure young wizard lady," he proudly replies.

"Are we supposed to believe that throughout your amazing artistic life you never used your wizardry powers?" interjects Firee with a doubtful tone.

"That's absolutely true," Houdini replies.

"What's the point?" is Reddish's opinionated question. "Real wizards do not use their powers in the mundane world," Houdini cryptically says.

"Why?" Reddish presses.

"We would disrupt daily life and the societal beliefs of mortals," the wizard says.

"Besides, what's the challenge, effort, hardship, and value of life performers without sweat and tears?" the magician says.

"Your wisdom is invaluable, Mr. Houdini, but I am still confused about something else," says Checkered.

"And what would that be dear young wizard?" he asks.

"Why don't you use your powers here in this parallel world of wizards if you can?" presses Checkered.

"Oh no. Believe me that I do, but not when performing for others. Wizards won't be thrilled with me exhibiting the powers they already have themselves. They get excited and thrilled with me pulling off stunts and escapes like this using only my natural abilities and talents," Houdini says then adds, "In a way the same thing happens in the mundane world, the public is awed and applauds for the same reasons," he says.

"What about your acts of magic in real life?" asks Breezie.

"The public wants to believe in the illusions I provide. They want to be entertained, but deep inside they know that they are not real," he says.

The great wizard waves goodbye and followed by a small

crowd walks away.

"Not everything is what it seems," I recall aloud once more Kraus' reading.

Everyone nods in consent as we continue walking along the riverbank. Then coming from the direction we are heading we are regaled all of the sudden with a festival of lights. Ahead of us, they seem to be coming off ground level. The intensity of the laser beams into the night sky captures our attention. Their colors seem to cover the whole spectrum of light. Bright purples, reds, oranges, yellows, greens, blues all commingle and criss-cross incessantly across the firmament in what seems like a battle of swords.

They know the young wizards have arrived. They've been observing them all along. The dark forces of wizardry gather up in the clouds in the form of high-velocity wind twisters. The winds lash with anger. Impatience boils. Impotence hurts. They have no choice but to wait for the right moment. After the debacle in Venice on the old prison grounds, they are no longer allowed to act against the new crop of young wizards before they've completed their first adventure and reading. So they reluctantly lie in wait filled with pent-up anger, ready to exact revenge out of the humiliation they suffered in Venice.

The laser beams we saw earlier are coming out of the Louvre Museum's famous glass pyramids. Beaming up with light they seem like glowing diamonds with rays bursting from every carat. The closer we get to the pyramids, the more we have to partially cover our eyes. We enter the grounds of the fabled museums and are just a few hundred yards away from the glowing glass pyramids when one of the laser beams rapidly descends and in perfect synchronicity widens and opens-up forming a tube of light pointing at us. Now right in front, we have an intensely bright tunnel made out entirely out of light. Without hesitation, we walk into it. After just a few steps, the cylindrical walls start to spin. The rotation soon turns faster and faster. The entrance in our back is suddenly sealed with a halo of light. In slow motion, live images replace the light rays across the walls of the laser made-up tunnel. It is a real life-size time-travel movie about our surroundings playing at high speed. Apparently going back in time, in rapid succession we see the pyramids disappear. The pristine walls of the museum become dirtier and seemingly decayed, cars on the adjacent street become more and antiquated, trees and foliage change colors with the seasons at high speed, only horse carriages now adorn the streets. Finally, the speed of the movie slows down to a standstill and the cylindrical laser light walls disappear.

"Young wizards, welcome," says Cornelius Tetragor our trusted mentor and book antiquarian. He wears his customary long white beard and robe, "You are now back to the 19th century," Mr. Tetragor adds to our already perplexed faces.

"Follow me please," he asks and we follow obediently still trying to settle down.

In front of Mr. Tetragor, we see blurry air in the form of a door -a portal- he steps in with us in tandem.

"We are going to observe a few masters at work. Pay close attention. Take note if you want to."

We come out of the portal into a dark alley following our trusted mentor.

Mr. Tetragor walks briskly through a narrow cobble-stone street, we walk and trot just to keep pace with him.

"First we are going to visit the workshop of Mr. Bartoldi. He can't see or hear us. Nevertheless, please do not touch anything," Mr. Tetragor says as we step into a large depository.

What we see right in front of our eyes completely amazes us all. It is the real life-size face and torch of New York's Statue of

Liberty on the studio's grounds; that's when we see the artist at work.

"Young wizards, although Mr. Bartoldi traveled to America several times to seek resources to fund the statue's construction, he never got much interest. In the end, the statue was built with countless small donations from the French people. Bartoldi in turn gifted the statue to the US. The lack of interest for the statue was such that the pedestal was not even completed when the statue arrived in New York," Mr. Tetragor says.

"Why is he counting so many small bills?" asks Greenie as she observes the artist now counting money.

"Those are thousands upon thousands of small donations that he received from the people of France to pay for the statue," he says.

"Let's walk back to the Louvre museum, let me introduce you to a very peculiar artist," Mr. Tetragor says.

Once again we follow him into the blurry portal and this time we come out at the entrance of the Museum. No crystal pyramids in sight though.

We enter the museum and go straight to one of its huge and tall gallery halls. There are several painters copying or using masterpieces hung in the walls as inspiration. Mr. Tetragor points to one artist in particular who sits in front of a massive picture perhaps up to 30ft. tall.

"The painting is called 'The Gallery of The Louvre' as he is creating a mosaic of copied masterpieces from the museum on a smaller scale on a single canvas.

We all admire the enormous painting. It reminds us of the equally giant painting we discovered in San Marco Square in Venice. That one had a carousel of smaller images with a larger one in the middle.

"The painter you see is Samuel Morse, the inventor of the telegraph and the Morse Code," he announces.

"Before all of that success he was for many years a highly talented painter that struggled to make ends meet," he says.

"How do you morph from being a painter to a world-class inventor?" asks an incredulous Checkered.

"Both activities are driven by utter and unfettered creativity and imagination," replies Mr. Tetragor.

We walk the streets of 19th century Paris. Most men wear top hats and are dressed in dark and stark colors. All women look overdressed in bulky clothes seemingly designed to hide their figures and femininity. The rigidity and stiffness of the people can be felt all over. After a long walk, we enter another workshop. In it, a large burly man with a dense beard works totally absorbed on the figure of a man that is inclined forward while sitting. His right hand supporting his chin is supported by his elbow resting on his leg.

"The Thinker is the name of this famous sculpture. The artist's name is Auguste Rodin. The beautiful young woman working by his side is his apprentice and lover, Camille Claudel, as talented as him," he says.

In awe and wonder, we follow our fast-paced antiquarian mentor through the streets of old Paris.

"Is sculpting more difficult than painting?" asks the ever curious Greenie.

"It depends on the eye of the beholder, some will argue that it is infinitesimally more difficult because it is in three dimensions and there is no margin for error. For example, if the artist chips away the wrong piece of marble, the whole stone is ruined. Others will argue that the perspectives and depth achieved in something like this painting..." Mr. Tetragor says pointing to a familiar painting.

In an instant, without notice, we are back inside the Louvre Museum but we seem to be contemplating it from a distance. Soon we realize that we cannot see ourselves. So we are not really present. He has just brought us with the purpose of looking at a painting. A bit distracted we all come back to the sound of his voice in the background.

"As you all know this is Leonardo da Vinci's The Mona Lisa. Let's take a look at it from the left side angle," he says as we all do, "Now let's take a look at it from the right side angle," he adds.

"The expression changes," says Reddish.

"So, you see, on a one-dimensional surface the artist achieved something extraordinarily difficult," he says as we are back to the city streets.

"Young wizards, it's time to sit down to a reading and have an in-depth discussion about all that you've seen," he says as we are caught by surprise.

Once more, we are standing in front of his cylindrical store in the form of a tall tower. The sign reads.

"Antique Books for the Spirit and Soul"
(est. long, long time ago).

"Welcome to my humble store, please come in with me," he says as we enter once more to his peculiar store. We sit on our customary bench in the center of the cylindrical place. He then performs his usual acrobatics up the impossibly tall and narrow ladder. High up he searches for the book he is going to read to us. Then he comes sliding at full speed using his arms and legs through the ladder. With a spring in his step, the otherwise circumspect antiquarian approaches us and starts to read in earnest.

"The Luthier from Mittenwald"

In the realm of Violins, Violas, and Cellos,
there was once an art craft extraordinaire
-A Luthier-
to whom there was no equal in the whole wide world.
His name was Leo Schoeffer.
He was born in a small town called Minttenwald
in the region of Bavaria, Southern Germany.
His tinkering skills went way beyond crafting, repairing,
restoring, fine-tuning even stringing
any of those precious instruments.
His incomparable abilities
were not only in the quality of his work
but in his level of craftsmanship when working the wood
-which were both better to none-
what distinguished him as the best Luthier there ever was,
the fact that Leo could "feel" and "breathe"
the string instruments as well.

One magnificent winter night,
while attending a concert gala in Munich,
the largest city of Bavaria;
The Luthier observed attentively
that within the beauty and magnificence
of the music performance,
although not noticeable to the audience,
his trained eyes and ears detected
that something was amiss with the leading Violinist.
This anomaly was taking place in spite of
all that could be heard throughout the concert hall,
was the crispiness of splendorous masterful music;
It was the sound of Heaven and Angels.

And yet to the experienced Luthier
the intimate and profound connection
between the violinist and his instrument,
were simply not there.
After an "Apotheotic" grand finale,
the Fiddler and the Philharmonic Orchestra
were acclaimed at length by the public;
three times the curtain dropped,
three times it had to be raised to the continued applause;
Shortly after,
the ever perceptive Luthier
went backstage to meet his longtime client,
the leading Violinist.
"What's wrong?" asked the Luthier.
"I don't know, it's a mystery to me," Replied the Fiddler.
"Did you drop it?"
"No"
"Did you hit something with it?"
"Neither. As usual, it never leaves my eyesight
until safely stored away at home."
"Tuning perhaps?"
"Neither. It's perfectly tuned."
"Let me take a look."
With great care the Violinist handed
the centuries-old Stradivarius,
worth millions, to the only person in the world,
other than him,
allowed to touch his most irreplaceable instrument.
First, with deliberate pause,
The Luthier drew the violin close to his ear
while gently knocking -using a single knuckle-
every inch of the wooden surface.
He carefully listened to the echoes' acoustics,

resonating throughout the violin's inner chamber.
Next, using them as the palm of his hand,
he proceeded to delicately slide three fingers
over the violin's carcass,
feeling every curve, angle, and joint
of the invaluable musical instrument.
He did this with his eyes closed,
seeking and expecting absolute perfection
and smoothness in the old masterfully crafted wood.
When finished, The Luthier smiled at the Fiddler.
"Let me work at it. I'll find out what's happening."

The next day,
the Luthier returned the Stradivarius to the Violinist.
"Play it, please," The Craftsman asked.
The eager artist, fiddle-bow on his right hand,
his violin over his extended left arm,
quickly mounted the violin on his shoulder
and against his chin.
But just before the virtuoso started to play,
the Luthier noticed the discomfort on the genial artist,
once more.
Sure enough,
the moment the musician rendered a couple of notes
with his beloved instrument;
he stopped.
"Still the same problem. What's wrong?"
said the frustrated Fiddler.
With a benign smile, The Luthier approached the Fiddler.
"Don't move the instrument," the Luthier said.
With great care and deft touch,
the Luthier ever so slightly
moved the position of the violin

on The Violinist's shoulder.
"Now place your chin back on it," the Luthier asked.

The Fiddler did and his face was immediately illuminated.
Totally transformed,
he unleashed a 10 minutes solo,
releasing all of his repressed musical passion
and desire with fury and joy.

"What did you do to it?"
An exhausted yet beaming Fiddler said.
"Frankly speaking...nothing.." the Luthier responded.
The Violinist reacted with total surprise.
"But I still earned my fee though...
You see, I spent hours evaluating your Stradivarius;
besides minute tinkering, nothing else was necessary.
I concluded that the issue was of a different kind."
"So I went back in my mind to your concert performance
and your subtle discomfort," explained the Luthier.
"You noticed it?" asked a startled Fiddler.
"Of course I did,
I know your routine quite well by now."
"How did you fix...?"
The Fiddler began to say but interrupted himself.
"My posture?" he asked.
"Not exactly.
It was all in the positioning of your Stradivarius
on your shoulder.
When I went back in my mind to the concert
I replayed your performance
over and over again, until I noticed
the subtle change compared to the past."
"One tiny tad and you noticed it?" the Fiddler asked.

"That's right, the apparent mechanical correction
placed you in the right frame of mind
to cause the imperative symbiosis and communion,
the ONENESS between the violin and you,"
The Luthier said...Then added,
"In people like you that's the only way
how the superb, incomparable quality
of your Stradivarius violin
and your immense talents
come out simultaneously and in full display.
An ever so diminutive deviation,
just a tad,
is the difference between ordinary Greatness
and utter, unfettered and galloping Genius,"
concluded the masterful art crafter.

The magic words still linger in the air when Mr. Tetragor poses his first question to us.

"Young wizards, there is a common theme between all the experiences you've all had since parting ways with the Orloj. Together, we are going to explore them in search of the answer," the old antiquarian says, "Greenie, what was your takeaway from the encounter with the great escape artist, Harry Houdini," he asks.

"We have to know when to use the powers we have and when not," she replies with trepidation.

"And how do you do that?" the antiquarian presses on.

Greenie hesitates then a sparkle crosses and brightens her eyes.

"When in the mundane world my wizardry powers do not work, which is better, because in case they did, trying to use them will only see confusion and doubt on others. On the other side using them in the wizardry world is pointless if all we are trying to do is impress other wizards," says Greenie with pride.

"This type of restrain in the end means what Greenie?" he asks.

"That we should never depend entirely on our wizardry powers. We have to be prepared to act without them at all times," she says.

"Very well. Blunt, what did you learn from our visit to Mr. Bartoldi?"

"Great projects and enterprises require the support of many," I reply.

"But that's not enough. What else is necessary?" Mr. Tetragor asks.

"The enthusiasm, drive, and execution of a few even one that plows ahead regardless of the obstacles, reversals and against all odds," I reply.

"Excellent. Checkered what about Rodin's -The Thinker-sculpture versus Da Vinci's Mona Lisa. What was your lesson after our visit?" Mr. Tetragor asks.

"Both being masterpieces, there's complexity in simplicity in Rodin's The Thinker and simplicity in complexity in DaVinci's Mona Lisa," she replies.

"Wonderful. Reddish, what about Mr. Morse, what did you learn from him?" asks our trusted book antiquarian.

"There's plenty of opportunity to re-invent one's self in life. The key is to never ever give up on your dreams even if they are as farfetched as the idea of a telegraph was in the era when Morse brought it to life," replies Reddish.

"Exactly on point. Breezie, tell me about the Fiddler and the Luthier, what did you learn from the timeless fable?" asks Mr. Tetragor.

"Perfection is a delicate balance between talent, rehearsal, execution, and the instruments, tools, or devices we use to perform; and it only occurs when there is an intimate connection between the three," replies Breezie.

"Dead on. Firee, what is then the common denominator between all of these experiences. What have you all learned from them?" says the old man with the white long beard and robe.

Firee seems like someone that is ready for the question. Still shy of our imposing antiquarian, he only babbles his reply. "The common denominator with the Houdini, Bartoldi, Morse, Rodin, DaVinci, and the Luthier is the virtue of Respect."

"Why?" Mr. Tetragor asks.

"What all of them have earned with their talent, hard work, and tangible results from us, is our respect," replies Firee now beaming with self-confidence.

Our book antiquarian mentor nods with enthusiasm.

"Proud of you young wizards. I wish you the best the rest of the way," he says before vanishing in an instant.

We are back to the present right in front of The Louvre Museum's glass pyramid. Suddenly I feel the familiar bump on my shoulder.

"Do you guys need anything from me?" says Thumbpee with a presumptuous tone of voice.

"Why didn't we earn an envelope with a clue this time?" Reddish asks the diminutive man on my shoulder.

"The Orloj already told you in his opening speech. This time around the clues are all contained in the experiences you

had with the six astrological clocks you visited throughout France," the spec of a man replies.

"What about a new power, didn't we earn one this time either?" asks Breezie.

"Only if your performance was excellent as in exceptional," the Lilliputian replies.

"Wasn't it Thumbpee?" Breezie asks.

A smile slowly forms in the pasty white tiny face of my self-appointed conscience.

"Of course it was, of course it was Breezie. Exceptional were Mr. Tetragor words to me on his way out," says the diminutive man.

"Each of you now has the power to create an energy shield to protect you. If together, it will be in the form of a domed shaped shield protecting you all, otherwise each of you would be able to generate a shield in the form of a side plate," explains Thumbpee.

"We'll face danger soon, right Thumbpee?" asks Reddish,

"Sooner than you expect, Reddish, sooner than you expect," replies Thumbpee just before disappearing once again.

We are left puzzled, still standing outside the museum.

Chapter 3

"RECKONING AND FIREWORKS IN PARIS"

G uys, go invisible now!' I reason while switching to thoughts only communications, 'Now, let's bunch together and create our cupola shield to protect us,' I think.

Both ourselves and our protective shield become completely transparent. Covered by our protective shield, tentatively we start to move.

'Buggie where should we go next?'

Our loyal companion's annoying buzz generated by the incessant batting of its wings is exacerbated by the close quarters we are all in. His tiny laser points the way further from the River Seine and towards a wide street.

'Where does that take us, Greenie?' asks Breezie.

'There are several landmarks located very close by the general direction, Buggie is indicating,' she replies as Buggie to our great relief vanishes, 'The National Library, The Royal Palace, the Concorde Square but in particular there is also a place where a landmark existed; it was the old central fresh food market, called Les Halles; it doesn't exist anymore since 1971. In its place there is a mostly underground shopping center called the Forum des Halles,' she adds.

We all look at each other in complicity. Buggie in the meantime is back batting his wings furiously and his intense buzz confirming our gut feel.

'I guess we'll have to find our way to the old market,' Greenie adds leading us away from the river across the Louvre's plaza.

'We are headed now to the Rue de Rivoli, the wide street ahead of us,' she says as underneath the transparent shield we can only advance with difficulty and in a rather clumsy fashion.

At first, we don't see the fog emanating from the river. I catch a glimpse in the corner of my eye and when I turn, a wave of thick white fog is about to engulf us. 'Let's sit down and wait this out.'

At first, we can't see a thing withing the fog, then fluorescent flashlights and numerous pairs of infrared goggles come into view. When the first flashes of light cross our shield and literally pass through us, we realize that they can't see us. After a few minutes, when the fog lifts, in an instant we are in for a big surprise. We are surrounded by hideous dwarfs with long corrugated noses and floppy coned hats. Each pair drags an extended net canvassing the floor. 'There must be fifty of them,' points out Reddish.

A pair of gnomes are heading our way swiping the floors as they pull the nets. We are on the edge holding each other tight. The net is going to make contact with us, it is inevitable. I close my eyes and brace for contact. But nothing happens. What I see next catches me by surprise; the edges of the big net are sliding through the floor inside of our shield, even through the legs of some of us. 'The shield protects us, they cannot only not see us, but they also can't fish or touch us either,' I think and everyone smiles and sighs in relief.

Suddenly we all jump as we see the face of our nemesis the dwarf. He is shaking his head in frustration. For a moment he seems to be looking straight at us. But it is only an illusion he doesn't know that we are right in front of him.

Slowly the small army of dwarfs retires. Their leader blaspheming ad cursing non-stop. We resume our walk underneath our invisible cupola shield. Soon we reach the wide Rue de Rivoli boulevard. A few hundred yards later we reach the massive underground shopping center located where the Les

Halles food market was.

'A portal?' I ask.

'Would a portal transport us in time?' asks Checkered.

'It already did in Prague. We came out on the same place but 10 hours later,' I reply.

Everyone nods.

'Are we going back one year?' asks Reddish.

'Affirmative, to the 19th century again," I blurt.

'Are we all in agreement that we want the portal to take us back in time to this location in the old Les Halles food market?' Breezie asks.

We all agree. Next, as only one of us has the power to create a portal at any one time, each one of us tries until Checkered is able to do it. A door of blurry air is in front of us. But when we are about to do away with our invisible domed shield, Reddish sounds the alarm, 'Let's remain invisible, we have to close the portal the moment we cross through it, there's a risk our nemesis is watching and follows us through the portal.' We all nod in agreement. As I am the one who created the shield, I swipe my hand across, and through thought I command it to dissolve itself. Quickly and eagerly though still our invisible selves, we cross the portal.

The dwarf has been scouting the route from The Louvre to Les Halles back and forth for a while already. His frustration is growing once more. There's no trace of us for him to find. He paces through the premises. Then hovers over them. Numerous other gnomes under his orders do the same. Nothing.

"Are these buggers lost?' He thinks.

That's when he gets an ever so brief glimpse of our blurry-air door portal. Though in fractions of a second it is gone, the hideous dwarf smiles for the first time in a long while. He now knows the likely location we are going to. But it does not last long.

"To what year did they go?" he asks himself rhetorically as he knows that once more we have slipped right through his fingers.

We in the meantime stand in front of a glass and iron structure.

"Thumbpee we need your help," Breezie says.

In an instant, the minuscule man is sitting on my shoulder once again.

"At your service, what is it you need young wizards?" "Tell us about this place please," presses Breezie.

"Let's walk inside. Les Halles was Paris' central fresh food market. This spectacular structure we've just entered was built in the middle of the 19th century (1850s) which is about the time and era you are in right now. The construction of this iconic and famous structure served for the Paris market to become entirely a food market. It lasted for over a hundred years until well into the 20th century (the 1970s)," the spec of a man explains as we enter the bustling premises. As his usual self, without asking, Thumbpee vanishes in a hurry.

The scents, odors, smells, and aromas take over and hit us at once. A mixture of delicious sensorial pleasures with the intensity and rawness of fresh products. The colors of the vegetables, fruits, tarts, baguettes, meats, seafood, spices rapidly overwhelm us. We contemplate in awe the mayhem of people and food products coming and going incessantly. A short bearded man with thick glasses zooms by in a hurry. He bumps into Greenie and knocks her down. He immediately drops a large notebook and pencils he carries to the floor.

"I am so sorry young lady," the nervous man says as he helps Greenie back to her feet.

He contemplates us with curiosity, he is particularly interested in the clothes we wear as he observes them with startled eyes.

"Your first time in Les Halles I gather?" he asks. We all nod with curiosity.

"Well, you are right in the heart of Paris, at least for me. I call

Les Halles, "Le Ventre de Paris" (The Belly of Paris), let me show why. This colorful, vibrant, and aromatic place feeds our entire city and then some. Not only all the great gourmet cuisine (kitchen) but also the equally tasty and more mundane food served at the restaurants, bistros, and homes of Paris originate right here. Additionally, great artists come here to paint, others to write, like me. Let me show you," our friendly host says.

We see how a young man steals a loaf of bread and is immediately caught by a pair of gendarmes (policeman).

"That's a habitual scene and probably inspired one of the famous French writers of all time, Victor Hugo, to write in his book Les Miserables a similar scene where the main character, Jean Valjean steals a loaf of bread and is severely punished for it.

"Well youngsters it's time for me to go. My name is Emile Zola, I am a writer by profession and also draw inspiration from this bustling place; I am currently writing about Les Halles," he says before he steps away with the same quick and nervous steps that led him to run Greenie over.

I am left speechless. But I am not alone. Every one of us knows we've just met one of the great French writers of all time.

Outside the building I see Buggie hovering. "Why is he not here inside?" I say pointing him to the others. I walk outside and the buzz of his batting wings intensifies as if he is happy to see me.

"I guess you can't be flying inside of a food market," I say and his quick buzz rapidly confirms it. "Is there something you want to alert us or point to us?" I ask but Buggie does not respond. I ponder about it as my five mates stare at me with bemused if not puzzled faces. "Ok, ok, I get it. This time around we have to ask," I say and Buggie buzzes in what seems like an amused confirmation.

"Buggie, what should we do now?"

Our trusted companion reacts in an instant by pointing his tiny green laser beam to the floor. We all look down and see a small brochure. It has one name in bright red letters: "Montmartre" (La Belle Epoque, 1890s).

We all get it at once and Greenie reaffirms "That's the name of the artists' neighborhood in Paris. It sits on a hill in the northern part of the city.

"Portal?" asks Reddish.

The hideous dwarf and his small army have been looking for us throughout the 19th century. Moving across time, year after year, they've been searching Les Halles to no avail. His frustration has reached unbearable levels as he keeps on drawing a blank with us. Then as the hideous gnome and his entourage arrive in the 1890s, he finds the Paris food market renovated into the same glass and iron structure. That's when he sees Reddish, the last of us to enter the portal. He zooms towards her but by fractions of a second, he misses her. All there is left are a small bunch of sparkling stars hovering right where the portal was. Huffing and puffing, the dwarf paces back and forth cursing while he looks for clues. Thank God that I picked up the brochure lying on the floor. What I don't know is that just as we were leaving, Buggie dropped another leaflet on the floor for the Gnome to find. It had the name of the Palais de Versailles (The Palace of Versailles), throwing the dwarf miles off course to the opposite direction of Montmartre, all the way in the countryside.

Montmartre (1890s), Paris
(Early afternoon)

We are standing at the top of a set of steep wide steps, surrounded by a Basilica and a Church; from the hill we are standing on, underneath in the distance we can see the city of Paris, including the Eiffel Tower.

"Welcome young wizards, I was waiting for you," says Lazarus

Zeetrikus our trusted book antiquarian mentor.

We feel immediately relaxed and at ease in the presence of the tall lanky man with a bent top hat.

"Follow me if you please," he says while marching away with his usual long strides and fast pace. We turn around and follow him through a pedestrian plaza in the heart of Montmartre. We quickly run into a cornucopia of artists all around. Street musicians, acrobats, jugglers, and especially bohemian-looking painters everywhere with their canvases supported by wooden tripods, drawing inspiration from the postcard surroundings. The combination of vivid colors between the garments the people wear and the flowers all around us projects positive energy and joy. Mr. Zeetrikus takes us to a workshop where we see a heavy-set bearded man working on a canvas with the most amazing set of violet flowers we've ever seen, the amazing combination of colors leaves us in awe, contemplating it for what seems like an endless amount of time.

"You are witnessing one of the greatest painters of all time, Monsieur Renoir at work," says Mr. Zeetrikus.

We move along and he takes us into a coffee shop where we witness an animated discussion between a group of colorful characters.

"Ah! the new crop of young wizards," says an extravagantly dressed thin man with a long beard," Come, come over here," he urges us.

Something unexpected happens as we timidly approach the group of adults. Everything around us freezes in time, except for the six of us and Mr. Zeetrikus.

A gallery of virtual images appears atop one of the adults drinking coffee. "Young wizards let me introduce you to the works of the most famous French Impressionist and Art Nouveau Painters," says Mr. Zeetrikus.

"That is Mr. Monet," says our antiquarian mentor pointing to the dashing young man.

"You can scroll them with your hands," says Mr. Zeetrikus.

We do and an amazing assortment of masterpieces are exhibited right in front of us. One in particular catches our attention, a beautifully dressed woman and a young boy.

"That is -Women with a Parasol- it portrays Madame Monet and her son, it is one of his most famous paintings," says our mentor.

"That is Monsieur Degas," he says pointing to another young man.

This time the gallery contains an artwork that catches our attention, it is a group of ballet dancers gorgeously dressed, and they are all attentively listening to their instructor.

"That Degas' masterpiece is called The Ballet Class," Mr. Zeetrikus adds.

"Next to him is Monsieur Cezanne," Mr. Zeetrikus says. "We are regaled with a magnificent and colorful countryside landscape framed an imposing mountain.

"It is called Mont Sainte-Victoire," he adds.

"That eccentric man in the corner is Monsieur Toulouse-Lautrec," He says. Then, introducing a dancing scene in a hall, Mr. Zeetrikus adds, "That's a masterpiece called At the Moulin Rouge, a famous French cabaret."

"Now let me introduce you to Monsieur Pissarro," Mr. Zeetrikus says pointing out to a night scene of a busy and fully lighted boulevard. "One of his most famous paintings The Boulevard Montmartre," he says.

"Next to him is Monsieur Manet," he says pointing to a richly dressed young woman in the gallery of images above him. She appears to be a barmaid.

"The Manet's masterpiece is called A Bar at the Folies-Bergere," Mr. Zeetrikus adds.

We are still absorbing the masterworks exhibition when Mr.

Zeetrikus is once again on the move. We follow eagerly though still coming back to reality. Just around the corner with Paris in the background slightly underneath the small hill of the bohemian and artists quarters of Montmartre we run into our book antiquarian store:

"The Jester, Antique Books for all ages"
(Est. long, long time ago).

The door is ajar so we promptly step in. The familiar itinerant store we have visited in Prague and Venice has the same strong smell of old leather and paper. The cavernous and dark place is equally unkempt with countless piles upon piles of books everywhere.

"Young wizards we'll discuss your recent experiences at length. First, allow me though to read a very special fable to you, it highlights certain values as a shield against the human flaw of indifference. Here it goes:

"The Young Girl from Budapest"
The young girl walked the ruined streets of Budapest,
her ragged clothes and worn-out shoes
matched the hungry look and sad eyes drawn on her face.
A loaf of bread here, a cup of warm soup there,
were handouts barely enough to sustain her,
but not for much longer.
There was nothing left of the home where she was born,
just rubbles and debris,
where the magnificent residence once was.

She had no idea if any member of her family was still alive,
four years earlier she had been sent to a convent
high up in the Italian Dolomite Mountains
in care and protection of her aunt,

her mother's sister, the nun.

"Sophia, the war may soon reach Budapest,
you'll be safe with Clara," said her mother.
"Your brother will be staying with your uncle Alfonzo
in New York," her mom added referring to her father's brother.
"And the two of you? Why are you staying?
Why aren't we all leaving together?" asked Sophia.
"Because we have to protect our home
and your father's factory," her mother said.
"Besides, this may all soon be over,
in that case, we will bring you back right away."
"I want all of us to stay together here at home, mom,"
"I am sorry Sophia but it is not safe at the moment
for you to be here," her mother said with finality.

Early the next morning Sophia was sent by train
to northern Italy followed by a long automobile ride
to the convent in the high Dolomite mountains.
But not before a somber and tearful farewell took place.
Her parents and her younger brother Thomaz
waving goodbye were the last images she had of them.
All she knew was that soon
after she arrived at the convent Budapest
had been taken over by the Nazis.
She didn't even know if her brother had made it
to America or not.
None of her letters to Budapest and the U.S.
were ever replied to.

Four years later, the war just over.
Already 18 years old, a young adult,
Sophia decided to go back home

against the strong wishes of her aunt, the nun.

Now, finally back in her hometown,
she didn't know what to do,
nor did she have any place to go.
She sat for hours at the doorstep of her house,
the only thing left standing in the property.
She cried softly, her sobs coming and going
as waves of sadness and longing inundated her.
First, they came to her like a whisper.
She tried to focus and get out of the haze she was in.
"Sophie, is that you?" were the faint words she now heard.
Slowly, she lifted her head as if hypnotized.
The sight of her parents and her now grown-up sibling
did not register as first.
In a haze and fainting,
she thought she was hallucinating
as the three figures moved in slow motion towards her,
which in reality was literally running.
She finally reacted in a snap.
Her eyes expanded, her stare filled with primal intensity.
"Mother, Father, Thomaz!" she yelled.
Her lips trembling and her heart pounding,
Sophia jumped then ran with whatever energy she had.
They all hugged and kissed to no end,
the whole family was all together again.
"We went to pick you up at the convent,
your aunt told us you were on your way over here.
We know you were all safe but had a hard time," said her mom.
"We were incommunicado from the world mother.
During the last few months
there was hardly any food, coal, or wood," said Sophie.
"We didn't fare much better either.

Hiding in a monastery high up
on the Tatra mountains of Slovakia.
We lost everything, Sophie," said her father.
"No we didn't, we have it all, dad.
We have everything. We have us!"
said the young girl from Budapest.

A whole array of emotions is reflected on our faces. We are still processing it all when Mr. Zeetrikus continues his non-stop lesson.

"The six of you have witnessed and met a selected group of some of the better-known French artists. All of them are considered among the greatest ever in history,' our erudite mentor says.

"As different as they are to each other. Some being writers, other painters, they all have things in common. Breezie, point out for us what did you see throughout these characters that links them all," asks Mr. Zeetrikus.

"Confidence in their trade," he replies.

"And that's a consequence of?" Mr. Zeetrikus asks.

"Tireless preparation, discipline, and rehearsal," Breezie says.

"Reddish, what else did you see in common in this group of highly talented artists?" continues the old book antiquarian.

"Absolute focus on their tasks. Each painter had a markedly different masterful style that required zeal, a commitment to the highest level of concentration while preserving their own identity," Reddish says.

"What about you Firee, what did you see in them?" asks a seemingly pleased Mr. Zeetrikus.

"Creative genius, Sir. Through an awesome display of unique works of art. There was nothing ordinary about their work," says Firee.

"And you Checkered what commonality did you observe?"

says Mr. Zeetrikus.

"Soaring talent, Sir. The conversation we had with the writer Emile Zola about the market being the belly of Paris allowed me to not only to visualize the inner works of food in a large city but to experience more intensely the aromas of all the food around me," says Checkered.

"Which takes me to you Blunt, tell me young wizard, what is it that none of these iconic artists have in relation to life, the world, or others?" asks Mr. Zeetrikus.

I ponder about it for a short while trying to visualize each artist. Then I get it in a flash.

"Indifference Mr. Zeetrikus. Not a single one of them was apathetic to the world around them. When Mr. Zola pointed to the thief stealing a loaf of bread and how probably a similar scene observed by Mr. Hugo led him to write it into one of Les Miserables key moments. Mr. Zole showed how engaged and the level of sensibility and powers of observation these great artists all had," I say.

"Very well done youngster, Bravo!" Says Tetrikus clapping softly. "Amazing and flawless performance," he adds just before vanishing in a cloud of stars and lightning bolts. Once again, there's no hard-earned white envelope lying on the floor waiting for us.

We find ourselves standing on the side street of Montmartre - the bohemian and artistic quarters of Paris.

"Thumbpee..." says Reddish softly.

In an instant I feel the little bump on my shoulder and sure enough there he is, sitting as usual with one leg crossed and a hand supporting his chin.

"Yes Reddish, how can I help you?" the spec of a man says distractedly.

"Aren't you forgetting something Lilliputian man?" she asks.

"And what would that be...?..Ajah! Of course, of course, my

apologies," he blurts out all tangled in his own tail, "If you all explicitly express the desire to do so, even through walls, you all now have the ability to see if people are infected with a virus," Thumbpee says before vanishing once more.

"Let's go and meet the Orloj, we better do it through a portal, we don't have time to waste walking all the way to the Notre-Dame Cathedral," says Checkered.

"With what purpose?" asks Breezie.

"Right, we better have a good reason. Remember what he said," says Firee.

"We have a crucial subject to talk to him about," says Greenie.

"And what would that be?" I ask.

"The mystery of the six astrological clocks across France," Greenie says.

"And the non-existing astrological clock of Paris as well," adds Checkered.

"I guess we have to get back to him the same way we accessed this parallel version of Paris," says Breezie.

We quickly agree on the destination, and to go back to the present. Each one of us tries to create the portal and Checkered ends up being the lucky one. We all cross quickly the blurry air in the form of a door. On the other side we walk into the back of Notre- Dame; hands in front we all move forward until we run into the same transparent wall blocking our way. Using our sticky extremities we climb the wall and move through the roof until we find the same latch door we used earlier. Next, we descend and exit the parallel version of Paris. We can now see once more the massive translucent astrological clock on the Cathedral's wall. As before, it sits in the place of what normally is an enormous circular crystal window.

It has taken the dwarfs the better part of the night to hunt us. Finally, the hideous figure has a lock on us and lies in wait with his small army until we finish our meeting with the Orloj.

Chapter 4

"MEETING THE ANCIENT EXACTING MACHINE ONCE MORE"

The thunderous voice always rattles us. "Young wizards, you've been making great progress on your quest. to become master wizards," he says, "But I don't want to detain you too long; but tell me, how can I be of help?" he says as both Thumbpee sitting on my shoulder, and Buggie hovering in the buzzing in the background, make themselves present.

"Orloj, you are located in the parallel Paris," states Checkered.

"You are right, I am in a place that lies between the real and the other Paris," the Orloj says.

"We are trying to make sense of the six astrological clocks we visited and the virtual one you currently inhabit," continues Checkered.

"Well, that's for you all to figure out. I can't help you on that," the exacting time measuring machine says.

"Is there anything you can tell us about the six clocks and you?" unfazed Reddish presses on.

"All I can tell you is that the clues of this year's quest all lie on your experiences with the six clocks. Pay close attention to the commonalities and differences between them," he says.

We remain motionless and pensive while remembering our visits to the clocks.

"One more thing young wizards, things are about to get a lot nastier for you. Be aware of the skies, the roofs, and poorly lit sidewalks," he adds.

Startled, we absorb his every word and try to discern the implications.

"By the way one of your opponents, the hideous dwarf has made the terrible and forbidden act of going after you in my proximity. I'll be taking care of him shortly. In the meantime, exit the cathedral from the opposite end you came in. Let me caution you though. The forces that menace you now are equally determined to make you fail. But they are far more powerful and devious than those you've so far been facing," he warns before going away.

Chapter 5

"FACING DARKNESS, FEAR AND DESPAIR"

We walk to the opposite end of the cathedral but we quickly find out that going in this direction the transparent wall is inside the church main chamber. The six of us climb through it expecting to find a roof at the height we found earlier outside. Wrong. We are close to ceiling level 200ft. high when we reach the roof of the transparent wall. As we are inside the enclosed wall, we move while hanging like bats, from our sticky extremities, as we search a door latch to exit it. Once again we find the latch by way of our tactile skills. Checkered literally finds it by touching it while sliding her hands across the surface. She pushes it up and we exit the enclosed invisible structure once more. That's when we hear the terrifying scream. Shocked, we see from afar as the dwarf and a large number of other small men are being sucked upstream inside of a fast spinning twister. We see little legs, arms, and faces rotating at full speed until we lose them.

"That's what happens when someone angers the Orloj," I say as we all swallow hard into our sudden dry throats.

"Guys we have to move on," I say putting on a brave face.

"Buggie," says Greenie calling our flying companion with an endearing tone.

The annoying buzz of the airborne bug furiously batting his

tiny wings makes itself present right away.

"Where should we go next?" asks Greenie.

Buggie hovers forward and we promptly follow. This time we head out of the "Île de la Cité" (the island of the city) through the opposite end. Next we cross a small bridge and turn left on a narrow street, its sign reads: "Quai de Gesvres." I notice that Buggie's tiny green laser beams straight forward. In the distance, we see that the illuminated Eiffel Tower is glowing. Then it happens...First, a single ray of light shoots right into the night sky and the firmament. It is quickly followed by a second one then a third. We stand watching in awe when the thick and impossibly long columns of light are each suddenly coated with a different color.

"That's my country's flag," says Firee pointing to the green, white and brown colors of the Indian flag.

"And that's now mine!" says Greenie reacting to the bright and shiny Red, White and Green colors of the Lebanese flag.

"Oauuu, that's my flag!" says Breezie in a rare sign of emotion to the red color with a touch of yellow of the Chinese flag.

"South Africa painted in the night of Paris," says Checkered proudly to her flag's plethora of colors in the sky as black, gold, green, white, chili red and blue all line up in the sky.

"My country's flag, what a joy!" says a highly exalted Reddish when facing the red and yellow colors of the Spanish flag in the night sky.

As for me, a knot forms quickly on my throat at the sight of America's flag. I can barely articulate a word and I proudly salute the red, white, and blue colors of my home country's flag… "Awesome!" I say.

The powerful beams now turn on and off as they switch

colors between flags in rapid succession.

"The other city, the parallel Paris celebrates and rejoices your presence, young wizards, be grateful; they seldom welcome newcomers in this way, in fact for many there is never a welcome at all," says Mrs. V. out of the blue. We turn around and look for her, but all we see is the set of twisting, ragged, colorful clothes flapping as they zoom through the air. Just for the briefest of moments, it stops as if making contact with us and making sure that we have duly noted her presence and that her point has been properly taken. Instinctively we all nod and she's gone in the blink of an eye.

Buggie's buzz brings us back to reality. He hovers a bit further into a wide and very elegant street, the sign reads: "Boulevard Saint-Michel". His green laser beam now points ahead slightly to the left.

"Those are Les Jardin Du Luxembourg (The gardens of Luxembourg) that's where he is sending us," points out Breezie.

Sure enough when we turn around, once more, our flying bug is gone.

The dark forces of the occult arts gather in the clouds, ready to strike and bring havoc and failure to the young wizards.

Supercharged lightning bolts explode within the cumulus nimbus. Repressed anger and obsession with seeking revenge the high-winds whip and lash finally ready to strike. They'll bring those irreverent youngsters and avalanche of hardship and fear, the likes they have never seen before.

Highly spirited we head towards the intended direction. Still reeling about it I peek back at the Eiffel tower to enjoy our flag's spectacular light show. That's when I see it. A dark cloud, more like a swarm approaching the illuminated tower at high speed. In a matter of seconds, the tower and its light beams are at first darkened then totally covered to the point that I cannot see either any longer. Then I realize that the same thing is happening to the building adjacent to it. It is moving forward.

"Guys, turn around now," I say and everyone contemplates the rapidly advancing massive cloud, darkening the skies and the city.

"It's heading our way. Run!" says Breezie.

We stampede down the boulevard Saint-Michael trying to get to the intended gardens, but it is to no avail, just short of our destination, we are engulfed by a dense and black fog. We get a hold of each other and do not move at first. Slowly visibility comes back but it is limited. The city air seems to be impregnated by a dirty, dark cover.

"Thumbpee, we need you," I say and in an instant, I feel the bump on my shoulder.

"How can I help you guys?" he says in a circumspect tone.

"What's going on?" I ask.

"All I can tell you is that the swarm cloud that covers you is in part a portal that brought you back to the year 1917," he says.

"Why that year? What's happening?" asks a nervous Breezie.

"The rest you have to figure out all by yourselves, now if you all excuse me, at this time I've got to go," the diminutive man says before vanishing in an instant.

"He never ever announces his departure," I note.

"Much less in a polite fashion," Checkered adds.

"It surely means something we need to figure out," Reddish says.

"He certainly was in a hurry," says Greenie.

"Besides the obvious, he meant two things: First his hasty departure is perhaps his way of alerting us that we are facing serious imminent danger and that he is not going to be able to help us," says Firee with his accurate analytical mind.

Tentatively at first, we start to walk heading in the same direction. Visibility is perhaps 20ft. at best. We notice that the few people we cross in the street not only keep their distance but their faces are covered mostly with heavy scarves, handkerchiefs or pieces of cloth. As we run into more and more people, a very bad feeling starts building up in my stomach.

"We are surrounded by sick people," Reddish says outing the elephant in the room.

"Not everyone but most," I say as people across the street also register on me as carriers of a disease.

"Guys cover your faces, do not get close to anyone or touch anything," says Firee.

"Where did you come up with that?" asks Breezie in contempt.

"I read it. That's part of how the world dealt with a pandemic virus in the early 2020s," Firee replies, "by the way; we can remain close to each other. I refer to distancing anyone else," he adds.

Rattled and out of fear we all find a way to cover our faces in our backpacks. Breezie and Reddish wear bandanas. I find a very British pair of handkerchiefs my father must have sneaked in my pack. I wear one and lend the other to Checkered. Greenie and Firee wear contraptions that I can't or prefer not to figure out where they got them from.

When we walk into Les Jardin Du Luxembourg we find pandemonium. There are countless improvised tents everywhere; lines of people in pain waiting to get in, some standing, some in wheelchairs; again and again they are bypassed by those brought in stretchers; nurses walk out and in, doctors as well from the makeshift hospitals.

"Spanish Influenza," says Firee.

"What are you exactly talking about, Firee?" I ask rhetorically.

"We have landed in the middle of a pandemic that affected the whole world starting in 1917, it is commonly believed that it started in Spain," says Firee.

We hear coughing, moaning and wailing non-stop. "Guys, should we get out of here?" asks Greenie.

We all look at each other and don't know what to do at first.

"If the whole city and most of the people are infected, there's not much of a difference. Besides, we have been diverted here for a reason," says Checkered.

We walk further into the gardens until we run into a small contingent of raggedy-looking characters.

"Welcome young wizards, we are your hosts while you visit Les Jardin du Luxembourg,"

Their old clothes hang loose; their wrinkled faces look totally worn out; each is missing at least one extremity; teeth, eyes, legs or arms. Their eyes though are fierce and fearless.

They all extend their hands to greet us. Weary and cautious we stare at them with puzzled eyes while maintaining distance.

"We are here to guide you through this place," the oldest who's dressed like a pirate says.

We hear but still wait.

"There's much to be learned about what's taking place around you," a heavy-set lady wearing gypsy's clothes says.

"Let's hear it then," says Breezie while we all remain safely at a distance.

"If you care to accompany us, we will gladly do so," the old man says swinging his arm in an arc as a welcoming gesture.

"I don't know, so far in the three quests -including this one, we've always invited ourselves into every place and situation; because each time we have been invited to anything, it has turned out into a mistake and trouble," I add.

Our friendly and smiley hosts' body language seems to be tensing and with it our level of weariness as well.

'There's no reason for them to be impatient,' I think for everyone to hear.

'I see it, I see it,' thinks Greenie.

'There is a transparent and compact bunker in front of us, our purported hosts are all inside of it,' Checkered thinks.

'That's why they have not made any effort to move forward. They want us to step inside,' Breezie thinks, 'These sets of extravagant folks surely don't have anything good in store for us,' she adds.

'I say we go invisible right now,' I think and we do so in an instant.

When they suddenly lose sight of us, the friendly stares of our fake hosts are quickly replaced by sheer anger and venom. Within seconds the bunker and its occupants disappear. None of us takes the initiative to be visible again, at least for the moment.

'We are not here simply for a visit," says Reddish, 'We have to ask ourselves why we are here?' she adds.

'I believe that we are here to see beyond the obvious,' says Firee philosophically.

'Explain yourself, I don't get it,' says Greenie.

'I see what Firee is getting at. We can now see if people are infected. This means that we should be able to see the virus itself,' adds Firee, 'But we have to explicitly express our desire to see it,' adds Greenie now getting it.

Following her suggestion, we all express the wish. The result is immediate.

'Guys, look up at the trees,' says a panicky Reddish.

Countless pairs of eyes surround us. The silhouettes are downright scary. Horrible figures of all sizes with tails and the shape of gargoyles. They are not moving but seem to be attentively watching and observing it all.

'They may be looking for us,' points out Breezie. 'If that is so, they don't know where we are,' I say.

'Let's go back to Firee's point, what is expected of us here; I agree with him, this isn't a sightseeing tour,' I add.

'Evil, pain, and suffering all present in one place,' I note.

'What about help?' asks Checkered, 'What about if the whole exercise is about us asking; How can we be of help?' she adds.

The realization hits us all at the same time.

Surrounded by a city infested with a deadly virus. 'But how can we assist?' asks an anxious Greenie.

'Let's ask for help ourselves; Thumbpee we need you, but only if you have the ability to be invisible and talk through thoughts,' she pleads.

It doesn't take long for the -now invisible to others- spec of a man to be seated on my shoulder, 'of course I do Greenie, am I not wizard myself after all?' he thinks aloud for all of us to hear, 'Young wizards, you know very well that I can't help you figure out this situation,' he thinks.

'We understand that very well,' I say.

Thumbpee nods seemingly satisfied with my words and just as we are resigned for him to vanish, the diminutive man surprises us.

'But I concede that the question you are posing is different; How can you be of help? That's an interesting question. Certainly noble, altruistic, and good-hearted. But words are not enough; What about you helping this city to get rid of this virus?' He ponders while wearing a big wide smile.

'But how?' asks Reddish.

'Again young wizards, that's for you to figure it out,' our spec of a man thinks before vanishing once more.

As we move through the Luxembourg gardens, the pandemic mayhem and suffering are unbearable and hit us even harder. We seem to be moving through minefields as we avoid the floating red specs of virus. They seem to be everywhere. On the trees, the beaches, the floor, the grass. Then from people's mouths as they talk or cough, we see the tiny clouds filled with red particles being expelled and spread through the air. We are surrounded by the deadly particles! As we approach the center of the park, the air and our surroundings are contaminated so we use our power to create our invisible shield in the form of a dome.

'Couldn't all of these particles be sucked away by a giant vacuum?' thinks Breezie through what first appears to be a grandiose and crazy idea. We all look at him incredulously until out of the blue his idea triggers another one in me.

"I got it! We'll use wizardry to create or conjure a spell that sucks all the particles away," I say opening a Pandora's Box.

The other five now all look at me, their eyes sparkling with excitement. We all know that a new door has been opened for us to start tinkering and exploring our powers. I decide to press the subject.

'Thumbpee how do we create a spell?' I think invoking our guide and companion's presence.

Strangely enough, nothing happens. For the first time since we met him, the diminutive man does not show up. Thinking we've crossed the line and he can't help us, we are at first disappointed then concerned. But just as we are about to give up on him, we are in for a big surprise.

"Young wizards, what a wonderful journey of discovery you are all experiencing. I am delighted with your progress," says our sweet and grandmotherly mentor; book antiquarian Lucrecia Van Egmond, "you've all reached a crucial point in your quest for master wizardry. In order for you to create a spell - your first spell I should say- you need the help of one your mentors, in this case me," she adds, "Let's move to my store, shall we?" she says. Then as it's her usual custom, with the sweep of her right hand, Mrs. Van Egmond creates a portal and eagerly we all walk, behind her, through it. Stepping out we now face the Luxembourg garden from afar. We are standing on an elegant street, the sign reads: Rue du Vaugirard. Though with less density as in the gardens, the air and our surroundings are still heavily populated with the virus' red particles. We follow our mentor and after a short walk, we run into a vast Louis XIII building. It has a plaque: Institute Pasteur.

Institute Pasteur
(Souscription Publique 1888)

"Young wizards, the type of spell you want to construct requires a noble purpose. Fittingly, for this year's quest, my itinerant store is located at this institute which has played such a crucial role in humanity's health. The Institute Pasteur was created out of the success of the rabies vaccination drive. Over the years it has contributed immensely to the world in the areas of biology, micro-organisms, diseases, and vaccines. It's named in honor of Louis Pasteur (1822-1895) the eminent French chemist and bacteriologist who discovered the principles of vaccination, microbial fermentation as well as the vaccines for rabies and anthrax.

Learning about Monsieur Pasteur and his institute's great deeds to combat disease places us in the right frame of mind.

Our mentor leads us to the side of the main building and we are pleasantly surprised once more. The sign reads:

"Van Egmond Antiquarians"
(Est. as old as this city is)

Next, we enter the neatly organized store knowing what to expect. Right on top of the same center table are the customary butter cookies and milk. This year though there's also food, all of which we gulf like hungry tigers in a couple of minutes.

"Let's see; the construction of a spell is not an everyday event. There are spells in existence for every imaginable desire a wizard may have, those you'll have to learn and memorize so you know what to invoke and when," Mrs. van Egmond says.

She pages through an enormous book while continuing to dissert about spells.

"A legitimate wizard should be able to create a spell in a brief moment," she continues, "The very first thing you do is visualize in great detail what it is that you wish for, then look for the keywords that best express your desire, she adds.

"Latin words?" I ask.

"Yes, that's the universal language for spells and conjures. Although you may find, according to the wizard or witch, all sort of dialects and death languages; but the historical consensus is a bastardized Latin. So it is more about the spell sounding Latin than actually being the language per se," she adds, "so, you want to vacuum the virus?" she asks.

"Yes!" I reply with confidence.

"Alright then; Firee search the verb "to aspirate" on the spell's book," Mrs. van Egmond says.

"Haustri" Firee replies.

"Now look for the words Pandemic, and virus," she asks.

"Pandemus, virum" Firee answers.

"Search the word city," she asks.

"Urbi," says Firee.

Mrs. van Egmond thinks for a couple of seconds then continues.

"If the spell is not correctly built or is incomplete, it may not work at all or cause unintended consequences," she says.

Mesmerized we absorb every word and every gesture from our endearing mentor.

"Young wizards now try any combination of the keywords from Firee," Mrs. van Egmond says.

"Before you start, let me show you the right way to formulate a spell if you are not sure if it works or whether it is suitable to your wish; first of all when not sure, never cast the spell right away. In order to build the right words, you do this without expressing the desire of what you want; when you do this the words you select will form a phrase floating in front of your eyes. At that point, you'll describe -not expressing your wish- what the spell is supposed to be for. If the spell works it'll stay in the air floating and blinking in front of you. If on the other hand the spell is wrong, once you describe what it is for, the floating letters will disappear," says Mr. van Egmond.

"Urbe haustri," tries Firee but all the letters disappear.

"Urbe haustri virum," Greenie tries but also fails.

The rest of us have the same result when we try.

"Perhaps because it is such a massive undertaking, we have to emphasize our wish as part of the spell," I say but everyone looks at me with lost stares. No one gets it. I ignore them, determined I page through the spell book until I find it.

"Desideratum, that word for wish in Latin," I say, "Try it now Checkered."

"Desideratum urbe pandemus virum haustri," she says and to our total amazement, the words all remain in place floating in front of us.

"Congratulations, now it's time to put your brand new spell to work," Mrs. van Egmond says.

We walk to the back of her store and exit behind her through the customary portal. It comes as a total surprise when we find ourselves standing, together with our grand- motherly mentor, in a thick white cloud atop the city of Paris. We are high enough to overlook the city from end to end.

"Say it! All you say it in unison," Mrs. Van Egmond suddenly prompts us. I immediately take the initiative on the count of three: ONE, TWO, THREEE!"

"Desideratum urbe pandemus virum haustri," the six of us exclaim together.

First, we hear the rumbling. Then we see the wind pick-up speed. Then it starts to whirl and twirl. Next, a giant tube made out of high-speed circulating wind is formed right in front of us. The cylindrical form is massively wide and vertically pointed over Paris at a low altitude. The wind suddenly picks up even more speed, that's when we see how the dark cloud covering the city is aspirated at a vertiginous speed. Our floating cloud descends even closer to ground level; at that point we witness first-hand how the virus' tiny red particles are being sucked from every surface as well as those floating in the air. The final and perhaps most amazing sight is we all see the virus' red particles exiting from the mouth and noses while being aspirated from every individual within our sight. It goes on for what seems like an eternity. Finally, the twirling wind stops aspirating it all from underneath and vanishes in an instant.

Almost instantaneously, Mrs. van Egmond walks through the portal and we follow suit; back at her store, she contemplates us with benign eyes, "How does it feel? Your first spell," she asks with pleasure.

"Amazing," Firee says, and all nod in agreement.

"Well, well, well; I couldn't be prouder of each one of you," she says pacing the floor, "We still have one more thing to cover though. Here is a reading fit for the circumstances," Mrs. van Egmond says as she begins to read in earnest...

"Together, As Ever, As One"

We are all in this together, we are as ever one.
Make it we are going to... physically distant
but closer than ever before.
We are going to make it through,
Together, as ever, as one.
It silently spreads... ruthlessly attempting
to undermine our Society,
threatening the way we live
as we know it, all at once.
There is only one problem,
for the virus to win,
and that is US!
It has to knock us down first,
but that can't or won't happen,
It is not even an option!
Because of You, Me, He, She, Them;
Because of all of us!
Stubbornly through great sacrifices,
resilient and enduring,
we are simply not letting the disease
exponentially grow around us.
You see...
Besides Your and Our Sacrifices,
As importantly...
Some of us do miracles by the minute,
Some of us are fearless warriors,
relentlessly attacking head-on an insidious enemy.

Our unsung HEROES,
We Honor and Salute You,
We are forever Grateful,
We are forever Humbled,
We are forever Inspired by You!
You are all,
EVERYWHERE you need to be,
ANYWHERE you are required to be,
FOR AS LONG AS is needed to be,
You are always WHERE you must be.
Laboring through the day,
Laboring through the night,
We all depend on you,
and do so with our eyes closed,
trusting without restrain and blind faith.
Incessantly putting yourselves in harm's way,
sacrificing it all for the common good,
you lose some but save many and much more.
You also light and lead the way for us all,
through this biological storm,
for our indomitable herd to conquer the disease,
stopping nature right in its tracks.
You Bring Grandma Back to Life,
You Preserve Grandpa for us to enjoy,
You Rescue and Save:
our Moms and Dads, our Sons and Daughters,
our Aunties and Uncles,
Our Nieces and Nephews, Cousins, Friends and Neighbors.
You Gift us back Anyone and Everyone
from the Jaws of Death.
As we Fight and Fight, Toil and Toil,

pushing back,
laboring without respite to defeat the virus,
not letting it grow.
We defend the Human Race with a single goal in mind,
To Never Ever,
Never, Ever, Ever,
Give-Up
on this precious Life we all enjoy.
It silently spreads...
trying to undermine our Society,
But it won't win!
It has to knock us down first, but that can't happen,
It is not even an option, simply because
We won't let it happen,
We won't let it be!
This abominable infection is in actuality
an existential opportunity,
Where,
We Love and Care,
We are Gentle and Kind,
We Feel and Share,
We Give Without Asking,
We enjoy each other's company like never before,
We communicate and Play better than ever before,
And suddenly,
We are infinitely more appreciative
of Everyone and Everything around us.
Additionally,
We learn and then some about ourselves
and each other, especially about:
Closeness, Intimacy, Empathy,

The Importance of the Small Details in Life
and How to Wake-Up from the "Haze" and "Spoils"
of a "Convenient" and "Comfortable" World,
conquering "Routine," "Boredom"
and "Lack of Purpose,"
once for all.
We also make up for "Lost Time" and "Time Apart,"
learn how to use it better and finally understand
what "Saving for a Rainy Day" means.
Through it all,
We Revisit, Reconnect,
Reunite, Reencounter, Retrain, Relearn,
Rethink, Redo, Retake, Reset, Replant,
Retry, Retry and Retry, Refine and Reimagine,
in other words,
We acquire the Gift of Restarting Life all over again.
We are all in this together,
We are going to make it through, together, as ever, as one.

"Firee what is the most important lesson you've drawn from this experience?"

Mrs. van Egmond asks opening the discussion.

"We cannot take anything for granted in life," he replies.

"Greenie, anything you want to add?" our mentor asks.

"Things in life can change in a hurry from great to worst," she quickly replies.

"Breezie, what's your take on today?" Mrs. van Egmond asks.

"We are all connected to one another, the pandemic we witnessed showed me that being part of society means that we are all interdependent and should always be asking ourselves how we can contribute to the common good of everyone," he replies.

"And you Reddish, what can you add?" asks our endearing Books antiquarian.

"I was mostly inspired by the doctors and nurses I saw working tirelessly while surrounded by the disease," she says.

"Checkered?" Mrs. van Egmond asks.

There is a pause as our mate is caught deep in her thoughts.

"Sometimes happiness totally abandons us in life," she says.

"How so dear?" asks a curious Mrs. van Egmond.

"Normally we earn or are graced with happiness as a consequence to the ways we decide to live and value life. But when tragedy or adversity strikes, our chances for happiness vanish," Checkered adds.

"And you just give up on it then. Any chance to be happy is then irremediably lost?" asks Mrs. van Egmond.

"No, no, no. Absolutely not. Witnessing the pandemic today, made me realize that in the face of adversity or tragedy, we fight. Yes, we have to fight for happiness. In those circumstances, happiness won't come to us. We have to go, search and fight for it. We have to make it happen within the circumstances. That's why in those terrible moments, we don't surrender, to the contrary, we go and fight for it," Checkered reasons.

Mrs. van Egmond's eyes are sparkling and full of wonder when she addresses me.

"Blunt, what has been the essential element in your experience today?" she asks.

"Selflessness, Mrs. van Egmond. We witnessed it in spades on the park with all the front-line workers," I say.

"And you all demonstrated it as well when the six of you

came to the realization of what was expected of you and asked yourselves how could you be of help? Then you went and put it into practice with concrete action," she says with a proud face.

"Young wizards, I couldn't be prouder of each one of you. My best wishes on the rest of your journey," she says before fading away wearing a big broad smile.

We are left standing on the sidewalk of a familiar street. The sign reads: Rue De Rivoli. In the distance, we see the sun breaking. It is the beginning of a new day.

"Why are we back here?" I ask.

Just in front of us is the Louvre Museum.

"Time to call our guides...Thumbpee, Buggie can you show yourselves, please," says an exuberant Greenie.

In an instant, the minuscule man materializes as usual on top of my shoulder and the tiny flying bug hovers next to us.

"Thumbpee, do we have to beg you every time for our new power?" asks a sarcastic Reddish.

"No, you have to actually ask if you've earned it," the spec of a man replies.

"Did we?" she presses.

"With flying colors according to Mrs. Van Egmond," he says creating the suspense.

"You guys now have the ability to connect the dots," he says cryptically.

And before any of us can react he is gone! We are all left startled with blank stares. For a while we do nothing.

Buggie, lead the way please," says Breezie finally reacting.

Our trusted flying bug points its tiny green laser beam to the other side of the street. We cross the street following it, then he turns right. Now we walk through the Rue de Rohan, followed by the Rue de l'Opera, and finally a turn to the right into the Rue de Richelieu.

"Ahead of us we have the Palais Royale (The Royal Palace) and right next to it is the Biblioteque Nationale," says Greenie.

Chapter 6

"DECIPHERING THE CLUES"

As we walk in front of the magnificent palace, Buggie continues forward. Soon after we are in front of the "Biblioteque National" Originally designed by Henri Labrouste, in 1875 and subsequently expanded by Jean-Louis Pascal with a staircase and an oval room. It treasures books from all the ages and from all over the world, as usual in the blink of an eye, Buggie is gone!

We walk into the iconic building. Suddenly the drapery of twirling colors zooms across the library's atrium. Soon after the familiar and comforting voice comes to us, "Young wizards use your six magic books and study the six clocks you visited. All you have is to connect the dots," Mrs. V. says with her words coming across the entire hall.

"Good luck!" she adds and with it, her raggedy twirls of colors vanish once more.

No soon she is gone, the entire library morphs right in front of us. The entire space is now divided into six sections with thousands of books each. Each area has a blinking, highly visible name, they are all floating in the air:

-Rouen,
-Lyon,
-Besançon,
-Strasbourg,
-Beauvais,
-Ploërmel,

"Where to begin?" Says Greenie sounding overwhelmed.

"Let's go to work. All of those books in the background will be useful to consult any additional information we may need," says Firee displaying his book worm experience, "Pull out your tablets so our own six books are available," he adds.

"What are we supposed to do?" asks Reddish.

We need to find the links between the six astrological clocks," says Checkered.

"What is the purpose of doing this?" asks Breezie abruptly.

"Clues, Breezie. Our visits to the clocks were not in search of a portal but in search of the book antiquarian that'd led each one of us to the Orloj. But Mr. Kraus only became accessible when we completed the visits to each and every clock. So all we learned on these visits had nothing to do with being able to get to the Orloj. All the information we learned was not by accident, and it all had a purpose. Now we have to decipher what are the clues contained in it as we'll need them for our final challenges," I say and everyone immediately nods in agreement.

"Did anyone take notes about what we learned about each clock?" asks Firee.

We all did in some form or another in our tablets so each one of us sends them to Firee's tablet. He quickly consolidates them into a single document and resends them to everyone.

"I say we split into three groups of two; Group one focuses on the key facts; both historical and each clock features, including the year it was built, who built it, its dimensions, dials, etc.; Group two focuses on links between the six clocks and our six books; Group three focuses on links among the six clocks," says Checkered laying out an action plan that we all consent on the spot. Soon, divided in three pairs we are all focusing on our individual tasks while pouring through our magic books, the notes, and the immense library we have at our disposal.

"Guys do not overcomplicate anything, the idea is to summarize and simplify things," Firee says, and everyone kind of gets what he says. At least enough of it.

An hour goes by and it is clear that everyone is saturated and a bit frustrated.

"Guys it's time to contrast and share our findings, who wants to start?" I say.

"We are going to formulate our conclusions in the form of clues," Checkered says.

"Our task was to find links between the six clocks and our six magic books," she says.

"To succeed at our final challenge we will need faith, hope, and clarity at the right time," Checkered says.

"Additionally, we will face the three fates that determine the course of human life," I add complementing her.

"How did you come about those two clues?" asks a perennially curious Greenie.

"We found the subjects in both the books and the clocks. We don't know in which way they'll present themselves to us,

only that they each will be part of a challenge," Checkered says.

"When studying the key facts and features of each clock this is what we concluded..." says Firee, "Automaton figures will be present amongst them a golden rooster made out of copper, iron, and wood."

"Astrolabes, planetariums, oculus, and orneriers will play a role in our quest," says Greenie.

"We focused on the uniqueness of the specs and features of the clocks. We reached the same conclusion Checkered and Blunt had; these items will be present in some form or another in our final set of challenges at the tour de Eiffel," Firee concludes.

"Many of the clock makers' spirits are restless and have remained vengeful for centuries," Breezie says.

"Only Temperatores (the clock keepers) will solve the conflicts ahead of us," says Reddish, "when analyzing the common links between the clocks, we found a couple of similar themes on several of them. The rumors about the original clock makers seeking revenge from those that rebuilt their original timepieces and Temperatores that kept them at bay as long as they were watching the clocks,' adds Reddish.

The moment our Iberian mate is done we hear the loud laughter and applause.

"Bravo!" says our eccentric mentor and book antiquarian Paulina Tetrikus. She wears her customary red dress; her normally circumspect face today shines with joy.

"Follow me please young wizards," she says.

Excited we follow her through the endless bookshelves of the national library of France. At the far end we see the facade of her itinerant antique books store, the sign reads:

"Tetrikus Antique Books for the Spirit and the Soul"
(est. as old as this city is)

We enter the enormous facsimile of an amphitheater, decorated like an "old-time" stage of another era with thick red velour curtains and an old wooden floor. Bookshelves are scattered everywhere.

"You've just connected the dots of your journey to the six clocks beautifully. Having said so, I've been expecting you for a while. I am afraid you may run out of time if you do not pick up the pace," she says while walking to her desk and lifting a heavy-set leather-bound book.

"Here is a scribble that will complement well what you've experienced today," she says just before starting to read in earnest...

"The Puppet Master and the Inquisitive Youngster"

As the puppet -master pulled the strings
with skill and artistry
the marionettes made the audience
-especially the children- laugh to no end.
In every one of his moves
he remained hidden behind the small boxy stage.
Through the puppeteer's vocal talents
the lively, jumpy characters went at each other,
arguing, singing, laughing, yelling, cursing,
and talking in high -pitched -Falsetto- voices.
Yet in the end, the feisty figures always made up,
to the joy and delight of the small crowds
that gathered every day to attend the show.
The puppet master traveled like a gypsy
in a never-ending itinerary
presenting his compact spectacle at tiny town squares,
through cozy Greek seaside fishing villages,
along the Ionic sea.
The primarily white architecture
on the tightly bunched enclaves,
contrasted harmonically
with a cornucopia of folkloric colors,
the verandas, balconies, rooftops, artful pots,
sidewalks, and countless flowers
painted everything with an air of delightful joy.
All of it was a perfect corollary of friendliness
for the puppeteer's act to thrive and resonate
with each Mediterranean spot he visited
and the appreciative populace regaled with his show.
One particular afternoon
as he winded down the show

a youngster waited patiently
for the old puppeteer to free himself up.
"Puppeteer, Puppeteer,
your show makes me really, really happy,"
the youngster said as the performer released his props.
"Thank you very much; your words are very kind,"
the street artist replied.
"Sir, I was wondering
how much control you have over your marionettes?"
"That is a very perceptive question you ask, young man.
But tell me, what prompts you to quiz me in such manner?"
"Well, it seems to me that although
you pull all of their strings for your puppets to come alive,
once your deft maneuvering sets them off,
they seem to have a life all of their own.
Even their voices seem to be beyond you.
It is as if while acting,
you split into multiple personas, characters,
and personalities that takes possession of you."
In the background of the deepening conversation,
string instruments could be heard
and animated Greek dances with even more colorful attires
took place it all blended majestically with the gentle sea breeze.
For what seemed like an eternity the puppeteer
observed the youngster with bemused but respectful eyes.
"Let me share with you what goes on behind the scenes...
Like in life, deliberately, consciously or not,
We, You, Me, Them, are always pulling some of the strings."
"But what we seek or aim to control never ever works
exactly like we want or expect it to be."
"You are right, sometimes things adopt a life all of their own
and that's certainly what happens in my case,"
said the puppeteer.

"Aren't you uncomfortable not to be in control
of the show and the strings you pull?" asked the youngster.
"No, I am not, that's how everything works and flows in life.
We pull them but we are not the strings,
we steer and drive them but we are not the marionettes;
we script and rehearse; we fine-tune, correct,
and fix them, over and over again, yet,
we are not necessarily the performance or the act itself,"
reflected the dexterous artist.
Then continued,
"When it's show time,
the artist, the creator and the string master in me,
all become secondary to the puppets and marionettes.
Those unruly, chaotic figures are
the ones who go and steal the show,"
adds the itinerant performer.
"So it is true then, while in the act
the puppets and the marionettes are really alive,"
the inquisitive youngster said. "In a sense yes!
At least that's the way you perceive it. That's what you believe."
"Yet, in as much as it seems that a puppet master like me,
controls all the strings and marionettes; Like in life,
that is only partially true; actually,
sometimes I am the puppet or the marionette myself;
Further,
depending on how we look at it, in a way,
once the show starts,
I hardly have any control,
not at least until the very end," the puppet master said.
"And what happens when it's over, are you back in control?"
asked the quizzing young man.
"Yes I am but only of inert and lifeless objects and props.
Without the show, the act, the public and the performance,

the magic is simply...Gone!"
the wise artist said, then added,
"As a puppet master,
I exercise control and pull the strings
while letting that what I manipulate
be their own characters and personas."
"And that's exactly like it works in life,
we don't control anything or anyone but us.
We can hardly guide, steer and rehearse the rest.
Life is like a puppets and marionettes show
with a life all of its own."

The air of our beloved antiquarian's store sits totally still as we all ponder and absorb her words of wisdom. Staring intensely at each one of us, she continues...

"You went about a difficult task with the right attitude and great organizational skills. I commend you for it," she says with a proud grin on her face.

"Now, tell me, in which way is the fable I've just read to you related to your experience deciphering the clues at the Bibliotèque Nationale?" she asks.

"In every way Mrs. Tetrikus; they go hand in hand," I say.

"Why?" the book antiquarian says.

"It's all about being humble. In the face of difficulties, adversity or obstacles, we go about them with determination and grit, yet without believing that we are in control of the outcome much less thinking we know it all," I add.

"What else?" Mrs. Tetrikus presses.

"We have to make the outcome happen while in the process we still have much to learn," Checkered says interjecting.

"And all this experience you've acquired, first deciphering the clues and then listening to the fable of the puppet master has shown you the perils of what?' our trusted mentor asks.

"Arrogance, Mrs. Tetrikus. How very foolish even dangerous would be for us not to absorb or understand well the fable you've just read," I say.

"I must say that I am very proud of each one of you. Remain equally focused and you will succeed in your quest," says Paulina Tetrikus before vanishing in a snap.

Chapter 7

"MEETING THE BURLY MAN
ONE MORE TIME"

We are suddenly standing outside the Bibliotèque Nationale on a glorious Parisian morning. To err on the side of caution we all become invisible and agree to go and pay a visit to the Orloj. We target Notre-Dame's Cathedral as our destination; Checkered turns out to be the one who at present holds the power to create the portal. We eagerly cross the door of blurry air looking forward to meeting the Orloj. Stepping out right in front of Notre-Dame we head immediately towards the back and the transparent wall that shields the ancient astrological clock. This until all of the sudden we stop as we hear his thunderous voice.

"Young wizards what a pleasure! Not that I need it but you can all become visible now," he calls us out.

The burly man with a huge round face, a twirling mustache, and a wearing a big wide smile, sits in a small coffee shop across the street.

Pleasantly surprised we turn around and join him.

"How do we find you inside of a city where there is no astrological clock?" I ask.

"My clock mechanisms remain behind the transparent wall, but while in my human form, I have no limitations during the daytime." he says in good spirits.

We pull a couple of chairs and we all sit around him. "How can I help you today?" he asks.

We look at each other in complicity.

"Orloj, we came seeking your feedback," says Reddish.

"About?" The time exacting machine asks playing coy.

"Our encounters with Mrs. Egmond on the virtue of selflessness and Paulina Tetrikus on the flaw of arrogance?" says Checkered.

"I see," he says pensively. A few seconds go by as he stares at us.

"Your execution has been flawless. My advice going forward is to not become overconfident or rush your decisions, you still have significant obstacles ahead of you to overcome," he says.

"Is there anything you suggest us to do differently?" asks Greenie.

"No. My words are only of caution. Remain focused and alert. Do not lower your guard," the ancient clock says as he stands up, waves goodbye with a half-smile and walks away towards the cathedral with short bouncy steps.

Parting ways with the Orloj feels uneasy and as usual, we suddenly feel like his sudden departure has left us empty-handed as we do not get a chance to raise the two subjects we came to talk to him about.

"He was intentionally vague," observes Firee.

"I believe it had to do with refraining himself from praising us too much. You could sense that he wanted to but did not want us to feel over-confident," I say.

Still seated at the coffee shop table, Greenie's exuberance snaps us out of the trance.

"Thumbpee, Buggie...We need you both, she says and in an instant both make themselves present.

"You forgot about our power." says Greenie teasing Thumbpee.

"No, I didn't. Once again it is never certain that you've earned it and you have to seek it, hence call me," the diminutive man says then pauses.

"So?" Greenie presses.

"I did receive high praises about your performance this time from Mrs. Tetrikus. Hence you've earned your new powers; you all now have the ability to deal with doubt and obtain positive outcomes out of uncertainty," the spec of a man says and not soon he's finished, he disappears in an instant. We look at each other confounded but know better that as the events unfold, our brand new power will make sense.

Chapter 8

"THE GREAT MATHEMATICIAN'S CHALLENGE"

In the meantime Buggie's buzz leads us back to the Rue de Rivoli across the Louvre. Once on the street, he points his tiny green laser beam to a city sign. It contains different city landmark destinations. In particular, the green dot is positioned over the name: "La Sorbonne, 2 km."

"That's the University of Paris, one of the oldest in Europe; it dates back to the middle of the 13th century," says Greenie our Francophile.

To err on the side of caution we are being invisible. We walk the now familiar route; pass the site of the food market Les Halles to our left. Soon after, following the signs, we turn right and cross over the Seine River and across the Ile de Cité with Notre-Dame on our left. After a short distance, we cross the river once more and enter the boulevard Saint-Michel. Far in the distance to the right, the sight of the Jardin de Luxembourg gives us the chills as we recall the pandemic and plague experiences that are still fresh in our memories. Thankfully, La Sorbonne is located just across on the left-hand side. Our anxieties are nevertheless erased when as we are about to step into the ancient and august university; the eternally curious Greenie turns around to glance once more at the gardens then pulls us to do the same. Totally freed of the pandemic pandemonium, the gardens of Luxembourg are resplendent, its beauty and open spaces restored and back to its magnificent and impeccable looks.

The halls of the university immediately absorb us. We feel the academic environment with students and teachers bustling all around. The place feels old, yet classy and well preserved. The old wood, leather, and paper scents quickly impregnate our senses. As we walk through the main hall, we see a curtain of blurry air right in the middle of it. We shrug our shoulders and walk right through it. On the other side, the hall continues and no change is apparent until we pay closer attention to the clothes both professors and students are wearing; they are from an era way back in the past. That's when we see the flyers posted on the walls all over the hall:

"The Methodical Doubt Challenge" Hosted by the great mathematician, Rene Descartes. Young Wizards! join participants from all over the world. Place: The Great Auditorium.

Excited we follow the signs until we find and enter the auditorium hall. It is enormous. Instead of seats, there are countless narrow rectangular tables with brass lamps. Five of the tables are already occupied -six to a table- by youngsters our age. We find an empty one and take our place. I am totally confused. 'These are all young wizards? How come' I ponder for everyone to hear remembering the yellow fliers.

"Thumbpee," I whisper and the spec of a man shows up immediately on my shoulder.

"What exactly is this? What are we supposed to do in here?" I ask as my five mates are all furiously searching for information about Mr. Descartes on the web.

"That's for you all to find out," he replies. "What year are we in?" I ask.

"1640," he says.

"But I see all our peers in the hall using their personal communication devices, tablets, etc.," Breezie says.

"Because like you, they all come from the future," he replies.

"How many are supposed to be in here?" I ask.

"You are all already in here, six groups of six for a total of thirty-six participants," the spec of a man says.

"I am confused Thumbpee. I thought every year there was only one group in every city trying to become wizard apprentices in Prague, young wizards in Venice and master wizards in Paris?" asks Greenie.

"That's the way it is. The groups you see each come from a different year in the future. This challenge only takes place every five years. Attending today are the young wizards' classes of 2027, 2028, 2029, 2030, 2031, and yours of 2032," the spec of a man says.

Ecstatic with bemused faces we all nod to him and among each other as Thumbpee smiling mischievously fades away. In a few minutes we all get a clear idea from the web searches we do on him, who Monsieur Descartes is as well as what his "methodical doubt" is about.

Then it happens, a very small and nervous man walks onto the stage. No other than the great French philosopher, mathematician, and scientist, Rene Descartes himself, in the blink of an eye he is seemingly staring straight in the eye at all of us, without delay he starts in earnest...

"Young wizards, today you will be facing doubt and uncertainty. In life knowing how to deal with doubt and uncertainty is an existential advantage. Do you fold and retreat? Do you fall into inaction when in doubt? In final analysis the challenge to be presented to you will require not only to deal but also to become comfortable with uncertainty and decisiveness. If you succeed, uncertainties will never intimidate or scare you and you'll never fail to make choices and take decisions in life," he says as an introduction.

"Let us begin then. For this year's challenge, I've selected six book masterpieces from three great French writer's. In each story, I'll pose a question that will create significant doubts in you," he says, "the books will be assigned randomly to each one of your groups. You'll be afforded all the time you may need to complete the reading of the books. Each one of you is to read in its entirety the book assigned to your group. No matter how much time we spend here, when we leave only one hour would have elapsed of your 24-hour quest to become master wizards," he says pausing this time to drink water.

In the meantime I can sense the excitement in the room.

"I've selected 'Les Misérables' and 'The Hunchback of Notre-Dame' written by Victor Hugo; 'The Man with the Iron Mask' and 'The Count of Montecristo' written by Alexander Dumas and 'Around the World in 80 Days' and 'Journey to the Center of the Earth' written by Jules Verne," he says sparking even further our imagination, "once done with the reading of your book, you are required to search, find and read summaries of the other five books. This is because you not only need to understand the subject each one of the other five groups is presenting but also, as importantly, because you may be required to participate in the discussion of the other five groups. Hence, collaboration between groups is encouraged," he adds, "when all groups have completed their reading, then we will jump in the realm of doubt," he says, "any questions?" he says.

"How long do we have to answer the question you'll be posing to us," asks Checkered.

"As long as you need to prepare them," Mr. Descartes says.

The great mathematician then performs a bit of magic.

All the glowing books lie on his desk. He then draws a translucent roulette in the air, it contains the six selected books' covers; then he spins it, when it stops he assigns the books accordingly.

"Class of 2028 your designated book is 'The Count of Montecristo'.

Class of 2029 your designated book is 'Les Misérables.'

Class of 2030 your designated book is 'The Hunchback of Notre-Dame'.

Class of 2031 your designated book is 'Around the World in 80 Days'.

Class of 2032 your designated book is 'Journey to the Center of the Earth'.

Class of 2033 your designated book is 'The Man with the Iron Mask'.

Then as if dealing cards, Monsieur Descartes swipes each book cover and sends it to the corresponding group. We each now have a glowing book suspended in the air in front of us. Still in awe, we don't know what to do.

"What are you waiting for? Make a decision," Monsieur Descartes urges us.

Firee gets it and turns his tablet on; we follow suit and do the same, the moment our six tablets are all on, the floating book splits into six and drops into each one of our tablets. The same happens to the other five groups of young wizards. The reading exercise turns into a several days affair. We read and work, day and night, until completing the book. Cooperation between groups occurs when each group starts reading web downloaded summaries of the other five books. We in particular consult each of the other five groups with pointed questions seeking to expand our general knowledge about the five books we didn't read in their complete version form. The multiple questions we in turn receive about our book, 'The Man with the Iron Mask', serve to put our detailed knowledge about it to the test. At the end of the reading exercise, the thirty of us have bonded into a fraternity. Pity that we all come from different years in time. We all know that except for a similar event, we will never meet again.

"Monsieur Descartes, we're all done and ready," announces Checkered who was unanimously appointed as the one to announce the news to the erudite.

The erudite Frenchman in the meantime has accompanied us all the way; answering every question or consultation, joining us during the meals, even putting us to sleep on the improvised camping beds in the corner of the hall. We've witnessed him laboring like an ant; writing, endlessly chalking up the board, and dozing off from time to time.

"Very well. Before we begin, let me clarify something for you that I am almost certain will surprise and even come as a shock to you. First of all, this is not a competition among you either as individuals or teams. As the name of the event clearly indicates, this is a challenge. And a very particular one indeed as it is a challenge against you both individually and as groups or teams. Second, this is not a test of your knowledge about the book either. Such knowledge is required for you to tackle the questions I will be posing to you," Monsieur Descartes says by way of an introduction.

We are all startled as every assumption of what was going to happen next, is all out of the window.

"As promised now you have all been thrown into a sea of uncertainty. Let's see how you handle it and how your ability to make decisions works when I immerse you into a sea of doubt as well," he says as every participant follows his every word with absolute focus and concentration.

"Class of 2028, on 'The Count of Montecristo' what would have happened in the story if Edmond Dantes would not have been able to switch places with the dead body of Abbot Faria on the canvas sac, hence would not have been able to escape on it when, as customary in that prison, the prison guards would have disposed of it by throwing it into the sea?"

The six young wizards of class 2028 debate for about 30 minutes then come back with a unified answer.

"The indomitable spirit of the character of Edmond Dantes as depicted by the author would have continued digging the tunnel for as long as it took him. Thus, he would've nevertheless escaped by also jumping into the sea. The rest of the story would have been the same."

"Anything the other classes would like to add," asks Descartes.

"He would have been older by the time he escaped because based on the Abbot Faria's calculations it would have taken years to excavate the tunnel up to the back of the ocean front prison yard.," says Firee on our behalf.

"But what about if Dantes would not have made it out of his cell?" presses Descartes.

"There would have been no subsequent story to tell. One can comfortably say that there would not have been a Count of Montecristo, hence no book either," states the leading member of class 2028 about the book they all read.

Without giving anything away Monsieur Descartes proceeds.

"Class of 2029 in Les Misérables what if Jean Valjean would not have stolen the loaf of bread, what would have happened to the story without him going to jail and subsequently suffering persecution throughout his life because of his conviction," Monsieur Descartes asks.

The class of 2029 pauses for what seems like an eternity but in reality turns out to be just a few minutes.

"Victor Hugo's timeless proposition is about an unjust society with great inequality and lack of opportunities. A society not fair to the poor with no paths to access wealth, a good name, or even love. The story would've ended being the same as the lead character Jean Valjean being rebellious by nature would have been trapped in another type of minor or trivial infraction -real or not- and would have been punished excessively as well with the legal system after him for life as well."

"Anyone cares to add anything?" asks Mr. Descartes.

"His pursuer, the relentless policeman, Javert, symbolizes the oppressing French legal system of the time," says a member of class 2029.

"In the end, it's not about stealing a loaf of bread but about extreme poverty and huge economic differences between the haves and the have nots. With those in possession of power and wealth sucking out all the benefits of society while protecting themselves by keeping the masses under control by being either economically enslaved or put away in prison."

Monsieur Descartes remains circumspect when he addresses the class of 2030.

"In 'The Hunchback of Notre-Dame', what if there would not have been a hunched back in the Cathedral but only a legend?" Monsieur Descartes asks.

The class of 2030 takes a lot longer caucusing. They seem to be in disagreement at first. A couple of their members whisper their arguments passionately. Finally, they seem to coalesce by taking a vote and are ready to respond.

"Victor Hugo depicts the dichotomy between ugliness and beauty. We learn that there always is beauty beyond or inside anything offensive or unpleasant to the eye. In the absence of the hideous character, the author would have replaced it with another figure equally ugly and equally deformed or disfigured, just in a different form, he would have still told the story in the same form."

"Obviously the title of the book would have likely changed as well to depict the new monster," points out a member of class 2031.

"There's also a metaphor in the book to the fact that irrespective of physical appearances, sometimes circumstances or people make a monster out of us. Then in others, difficult even the most challenging situations bring the best out of us. In this regard physical appearances do not matter at all," concludes the class of 2030.

As hard as he is trying, it becomes obvious to all of us that Monsieur Descartes is not only pleased but is also enjoying himself.

"Class of 2031 in 'Around the World in 80 Days', what would have happened if Phileas Fogg had not realized that by having crossed the international date line, he still had a day to spare to make it to London, causing him to believe before his arrival that he had lost his bet of circling the globe in 80 days?" asks Monsieur Descartes.

The class of 2031 seems to be ready for the question because they proceed to respond right away through their appointed speaker.

"Nothing, Mr. Fogg would have still presented himself to his club members in London to accept his loss and pay his bet. Jules Verne's book is not about the main character winning or losing a wager but about Fogg's journey of self-discovery where being beforehand a very rigid and monotonous man trapped by rules and stiff English traditions, he opens up to the world, life, and its people by going and experiencing it first-hand."

"Does anyone have anything else to add?"

"The main character regardless of the bet, by the time of his journey's final leg from America to London has already achieved his goals just enumerated," says a member of the 2032 class.

"The bet is only an excuse for him to embark on a daring adventure to explore the many different cultures and places the planet has to offer and to break from a narrow and sad life," concludes the class of 2031.

Monsieur Descartes now paces himself slowly; hand on chin, not trying anymore to hide his obvious delight.

"Class of 2032 what would have happened to Jules Verne's character, Professor Lidenbrook's adventure if he would not have found Arne Saknussemm's initials carved on the walls of the Iceland cave that eventually led him into the center of the earth?"

The 2032 class debates for a brief period of time seemingly as well ready for the question.

"Professor Lidenbrook would have carried on, nevertheless. His desire to reach the center of the earth was bigger than any particular obstacle. He would have faced though more uncertainty and peril without the markings and clues of his predecessors. But in the end, in Verne's story, he and his companions are the ones that reached the center of the earth, no one else."

"Any additional opinions?" asks Monsieur Descartes.

"Professor Lidenbrook never doubts or deviates from the purpose of reaching the center of the earth. What seems crazy to others it isn't to him, reaching his goal is all he obsesses about, he displays not only courage and determination but also self-reliance as he does not depend on anyone to reach his goals," concludes the class of 2033.

Monsieur Descartes now contemplates all of us with his arms folded while nodding softly. A big wide smile draws across his face.

"Class of 2033, in 'The Man with the Iron Mask', what if the man trapped in the iron mask would have been someone else and not the rightful king as he would have escaped to a foreign land?" asks the eminent professor.

It does not take us long to agree on an answer.

Reddish leads the way representing us.

"The story and its outcome would not have changed. The real king would have eventually made his way back to regain the throne as well. Perhaps he would have not experienced the same type of suffering and pain of being trapped behind a mask but the loss of the throne would have still been the same."

"Anyone cares to add an opinion?" asks Monsieur Descartes,

"The story is more about the lessons the king learns when out of the throne than the mask itself," says a member of class 2028.

"When he returns to hold the crown once more, he values more his role and has become more sensitive to its subjects," Reddish concludes.

Monsieur Descartes paces with deliberately slow strides. Hand on his chin he observes us all with satisfaction and pride.

"Young wizards, it's been a pleasure and an honor to guide you through seas of uncertainty and doubt. I must say that you've succeeded with flying colors and way beyond my expectations. I enjoyed every minute of this year's challenge. I sincerely believe that you are all now even better equipped and prepared to deal with those existential poisons of the spirit," he says then bows his head while waving goodbye to us all. And that's the last thing we remember as everything around us vanishes in an instant.

Suddenly the six of us are all alone in the auditorium; our peers and the great mathematician are all gone. That's when we hear the lone applause. There he is, our book antiquarian and mentor, the man with an unruly mat of hair, Morpheous Rubicom. He claps slowly seemingly enjoying every moment.

"Very well done! C'mon follow me young wizards, there is no time to waste," he says as he starts to walk.

In the University's hall, he leads us through the same blurry air curtain covering the corridor from side to side and floor to ceiling. Stepping to the other side, back to the present we continue through the university's main hall. Just before we reach the main exit doors, Mr. Rubicom turns right and that's when we see the facade of his itinerant store, the sign reads:

**"Rubicom Antiquarian Books about Wealth,
Fame and Love,"**
(Est. several generations ago).

We walk into his confined store. It is a very small space, with a low ceiling, yet saturated from wall to wall with books.

"I am eager to discuss in depth the experience you all just had with Monsieur Descartes. But before we do, there is one fable that I need to share with you in order to complement further your knowledge of the human flaw you are learning about," he says just before starting to read in earnest...

"The Troll and The Determined Youngster from Tromso"
The view from high-up at the flat-top bedrock, is stunning,
seemingly it goes on for miles and miles to no end,
underneath, deep blues and greens can be seen,
all depicting a perfect Norwegian postcard
of immense and sinuous water expanses,
filled with jagged bays and estuaries
-the famous Nordic fjords-
water channels framed by vertical
and giant mountains, on both sides saturate it all.

The youngster grew up in the long days and nights of Tromso,
located way, way up in the land of Vikings
not far from Nordcap,
the northern most civilized enclave in the world
before the north pole.
Today's effort to reach the top of the mountain
is the culmination of a long recovery
for young Oleg.
After his third birthday,
he was not able to walk,
not even move his legs any longer.
A bacteria they said,
had affected his lower extremities and motor-skills.
He breaths deeply inhaling with pleasure
the temperate air of the mountain summit.
He stands on both legs,

those he was told countless times
he was never going to be able to use, ever again.
"So you finally made it, Young Oleg,"
says with a thunderous voice the troll of the mountain,
his long-time friend.
Short, with a big head and a long corrugated nose,
wearing a coned-floppy cap
and "Tyrolean" shorts with suspenders,
the mountain troll is never this friendly with anyone.
To the contrary,
his reputation through a centuries old life is one of mischief,
havoc and mayhem.
But his relationship with the determined youngster
has been different from the beginning.
It all began inauspiciously,
a tiny boy of eight perhaps nine years old
at the base of the big mountain,
choosing not to take the cable car
but instead, to hike it up.
The detestable figure contemplated
the youngster's feat with disdain and skepticism.
'He could ride the tram for a few minutes and be at the top,
this boy is a fool,' reflected the mountain troll
while contemplating Young Oleg with leg braces
and crutches trying to walk up the mountain.
Why do you bother? You'll never make it,"
said the troll while standing atop of a rock
with his arms crossed.
The handicapped youngster barely acknowledged his presence.
"I may not make it today, but eventually I will,"
Oleg said with a big broad smile.
The mountain troll was truly impressed.
His mere presence, together with a hideous voice,

always intimated others.

But not this youngster.

'Who is he?' An intrigued troll asked himself.

That day Oleg was barely able to walk a few hundred meters.

But the next morning the young boy was at it once more
and this time managed twice the distance.

"Why do you torture yourself?" the mountain troll asked.

"I am enjoying the effort Troll, don't you understand?"
Oleg said.

"Not really," replied an incredulous Troll.

Throughout the summer Oleg continued to make progress.

Sometimes he didn't advance much in distance
or anything at all.

But he compensated with better balance and less effort overall.

What really amazed the mountain troll was
that when the long winter nights arrived
Oleg did not stop coming
and trying to conquer the mountain again and again.

Same time at midday everyday under a tenuous sun,
like clockwork he showed up and continued advancing
two steps forward, one backwards, three forward…

"What do you want out of this?" the mountain troll asked.

"To hone in and improve my ability to walk.

I am working on my skills and talent,"
said the by then 14 years old.

Oleg was by that time already able to walk on his leg braces
all the way up to the middle of the mountain.

As a matter of fact the crutches he had dropped altogether
from his daily life a while ago.

"Oleg, what is the key ingredient that keeps you
making this effort over and over again?"
the mountain troll asked.

"Focus. My concentration on my final objective

will not change or deviate until I reach
the top of the mountain,"
Oleg said.
By the time he was 16 years old,
Oleg attempted the ultimate challenge.
He took off his leg braces
but hardly could stand much less walk.
His by now close companion and admirer the mountain troll
was disheartened and pessimistic.
'I had become to believe that he was going
to make it to the top, but now?'
he mulled over at the sight of the helpless youngster.
Oleg was back to square zero at the bottom of the mountain
only able to walk a few hundred meters at the time.
"Are you a masochist? Do you like to suffer or be in pain?"
said an obfuscated mountain troll.
"Not in the least, to the contrary I am always happy.
My mother says that I was born
with an innate sunny disposition for life."
"Well, watching you walk,
it sure doesn't look like something joyful to me,"
said sarcastically the mountain troll.
"Talent and acquired skills driven by focus and concentration
are not enough, in addition,
I must have the desire and predisposition,
the willingness to sacrifice,
to endure pain and struggles
in the process of learning and improving,"
said the now 18 years old.
Today,
Oleg has finally walked on his own
all the way to the top of the mountain
atop the Norwegian Fjords and his hometown of Tromso.

He has done it, although with great effort,
seemingly to the untrained eye, like any other hiker.
"Oleg, my dearest of all friends,"
starts to say the mountain troll.
"What's your secret ingredient?
Talent, skills, focus, concentration, readiness to sacrifice,
and struggle are not enough.
What's the final magic component, the catalyst
to all you've accomplished?"
"Passion, Troll, I intensely loved doing what I did
and that made me pure and simply Happy!"
Finally, after a long journey that took forever
he gave himself the luxury of riding the cable car
down on his way home.
The beautiful autumn Nordic sun set in the horizon
as the mountain troll waved goodbye to his forever friend,
Oleg, the determined youngster from
the Norwegian town of Tromso.

As our eccentric antiquarian mentor finishes, I feel like I've just finished the longest of roller coaster rides.

Mr. Rubicom contemplates each one of us straight in the eye as if trying to decipher everything we his disciples are going through.

"Your adventure in the Sorbonne required you to listen and pay close attention to everything and everyone around you. You could not let your concentration and focus go not even for a second. I am glad to tell you that you did exactly that. Now you've seen the same kind of determination to succeed by the handicapped youngster from Tromso. In both his case and yours, reality was completely blocked for a noble purpose; but if there are no valid or good reasons to block reality, what would that be?" our mentor asks.

"Deafness!" I reply.

Our eccentric mentor and book antiquarian reacts immediately with effusiveness and enthusiasm. Each one of us receives a bear hug from him; visibly emotional, he is at a loss of words while he contemplates us with eyes filled with satisfaction.

"You excelled at every instance under trying circumstances and were certainly," he says, "you're now very close to your final set of challenges at the Tour de Eiffel. Stay the course and remain focused," he says before disappearing in the blink of an eye.

We are back standing in the Boulevard Saint-Michel. It does not take long for our two companions to show up. This time though, they come without us calling them.

"So we don't need to call you anymore?" I ask sarcastically.

"It depends. In situations like this where it is so predictable that you'll contact us, we may as well do it in advance. On all others circumstances everything remains the same; you have to call us," says Thumbpee while seated comfortably, as his usual self, on my shoulder, "and before you ask, the answer is yes, you've also earned a new power, with flying colors said Mr. Rubicom," says the spec of a man now more of himself than usual, "You now have the ability to sense when danger is approaching you," he says and vanishes before we can react.

His words create anxiety in all of us as they act as a premonition of things to come. In the meantime Buggie's buzz intensifies spontaneously. When we turn around, we find the flying bug pointing to the ground with his tiny green laser beam.

"There's nothing on the floor,' Greenie says.

We turn around and stare at Buggie. His tiny and green laser beam is intermittent.

"Does he want us to simply walk?" asks Reddish.

"That or he doesn't know. His buzzing seems to indicate that," I say.

"Thumbpee throw us a bone here, c'mon!" Breezie says.

Chapter 9

"THE LOOSE END PORTAL"

The slight bump on my shoulder indicates the arrival of the minuscule man.

"Guys, the place to go next is part of your original plan. You haven't been there yet," he says cryptically.

We look at each other quizzically but Firee's gestures signal that he got it.

"What else Thumbpee?" asks Firee.

"In order for you to reach your mentor, this time you'll have to solve a loose end you left open from the very beginning of your quest," the spec of a man says and is immediately thereafter gone.

Buggie is still around hovering aimlessly above us. Firee takes the lead right away.

"Besides the Eiffel Tower, what is the landmark we haven't been to yet?" he asks.

"L'arc D'Triumph," jumps Francophile Greenie to Buggie's delight as he goes crazy buzzing with impetus and maximum intensity.

We know where we are heading next though we still need to understand Thumbpee's second clue. But by now we all know better to be patient as eventually it'll make sense. We quickly agree to create a portal into our destination and Breezie turns out to be holding such power. We all cross eagerly and are immediately regaled with a great surprise.

The L'arc D'Triumph stands majestic in front of us glowing in incandescent lights. The center arc immediately stands out because of the blurry air covering it.

"L'arc D'Triumph is a gigantic portal!" says an exuberant Greenie.

As we get closer the blurry air is filled with images. We quickly recognize the six astrological clocks we visited. Additionally, there are three separate images of men totally unknown to us. In total there are nine images.

"L'arc D'Triumph's portal can only be used four times. Further, you'll only succeed if you use it in the right order," is the familiar voice of Mrs. V.

When we turn around we get a glimpse of the raggedy and twirling colorful cloth zooming away from us.

"Guys, time to put on our thinking hats," I say.

"We have to determine which four of the 9 images are our portal destinations," says Reddish.

"That's not difficult to discern," says Firee. We all look at him eager to solve the mystery.

"We have six images whose places we already visited," says Firee.

"Which means that since we don't know if they are useful or not, we must visit each of the three men on the images," says Checkered.

"And that means that we can only visit one of the clocks but which?" asks a confused Greenie.

"Yes, how do we know which one of the six?" asks Reddish.

"That's a more difficult proposition," says Firee.

As I've been listening fascinated with the exchange; I've yet to participate. It surprises me when the answer hits me so easily…"The astrological clock of Lyon," I say.

"Why?" Asks Greenie.

"Because it is the only not working," I say.

"What's the relevance of that?" asks Reddish.

"It is the single most significant difference between the six astrological clocks," says Checkered.

"Are the three individuals related to the clocks then?" asks Breezie.

"They must be connected to the clock," I say. "The clock?"

"The clock of Lyon," I reply.

"Why to that clock in particular?" Breezie presses. "Because it needs repair..." I begin to say but get lost in my own thoughts. The next words out of my mouth come out without thinking, they surprise even me, "Because they are likely the couple of clock makers in conflict. The Temperatore is who kept them at bay," I blurt out.

"Weren't they related to another clock?" asks Checkered as she consults her iPad notes, "Yes! here it is, they are related to the Besançon clock, not Lyon," she says finding the answer before any of us.

"The two clock makers are the clue to all of this, the writing is on the wall," points Breezie looking at all of us for answers.

"I suspect that we need to repair the clock, and they are the right parties," I say.

The moment my words sink in is like a curtain lifts in front of all of us. Our expressions denote self-confidence and enthusiasm but it does not last long.

"Where do we go first?" asks Greenie clueless again as we all are.

"The clock of Lyon?" asks Reddish.

"No, that'll be the last we'll visit," Firee replies. "Why?" presses Reddish.

"We'll go there to repair the clock when we have the people that'll do it," I say.

We've all reached a level of understanding of the choices we have in front of us.

"Which of the three individuals should we visit first?" asks Breezie.

"The Temperatore," I say.

"Why?" asks Greenie.

"He kept the spirits of the two warring clock makers at bay for decades. We need to persuade him to intervene and get the clockmakers to agree to work together," I reply.

"And which of the two clock makers do we visit first?" asks Breezie.

"We'll let the Temperatore decide," replies Firee.

"How do we determine from these images which of the three men is the Temperatore?" asks Reddish.

"By their clothes. Let us check the images together," I say and it does not take long for us to recognize it.

"Two are very similarly dressed, the third is dressed poorly, that's the guard," Firee points out with his infallible logic.

Instinctively our daring Greenie places her hand on the supposed Temperatore's image. The enormous L'arc D'Triumph's center arc becomes an enormous portal of blurry air; as we select the image of whom we believe to be the Temperatore, we walk through the portal; our destination is unknown. On the other side, we come out to a street right in front of L'Opera de Paris.

"What would a Temperatore be doing in The Opera house? asks Greenie.

"I have a pretty good idea, let's go," I say.

We cross the street and walk inside. The place is empty, there are no performances in broad daylight. A security guard approaches and we ask him if the building has a maintenance guy or perhaps a concierge. He answers yes but none of them are on the premises, he says. The idea all of a sudden hits me like a thunder ball.

"Is there someone that lives on the premises?" I ask. "How do you know?" asks the guard.

"Sir, we don't know; we are asking you." I say.

"Well, there is Monsieur Brandibas, the utility man."

The name immediately rings a bell. Firee checks our notes and nods, "Paul Brandibas?" He asks referring to the Besançon's astrological clock Temperatore's name.

"Yes, he lives high above the stage in an attic located at the roof level. He seldom goes out and works only when the place is empty.

"Thank you, Sir, you don't mind if we go and pay Mr. Brandibas a visit?" asks daring Greenie.

"Not at all. Besides, I appreciate when people ask; in order to get to his place here is what you have to do. First, go backstage, and you'll find a black security ladder, that will lead you straight into his loft.

Excited, we walk away with a spring in our strides. Breezie is the first one to throw cold water on the momentum we have.

"Blunt, I still believe that the assumption we have and adopted, may be wrong," he says.

"Why?" I ask

"We got the right profession of the man on the image. He is a Temperatore alright but of the wrong clock," Breezie presses,

"The Temperatore we are about to meet was the clock keeper of the Besançon astrological clock, not Lyon," he says.

"I know and probably the two clock makers are those that built the first two versions of the same Besançon astrological clock," I say.

"I don't understand," Breezie says puzzled.

"I believe our purported mission is to repair the clock. In order to do that we need specialists in that craft. We have to persuade the Temperatore to act as a mediator to convince the clockmakers to work together. We want to dangle a carrot in front of these men so they coalesce around a project. For example, repairing the Lyon astrological clock," I say spontaneously and surprise my five mates. By the time we knock at Monsieur Brandibas' door we don't know what to expect. The man that opens the door is obviously taken aback as he seldom receives any visitors much less a group of 14 years old youngsters with backpacks on their shoulders.

"Monsieur Brandibas?" "Yes?"

""We have a proposition for you," I say.

"And what would that be?" he says with an intrigued tone of voice.

"We understand that for several decades you intermediated and kept the spirits at bay of the two clock makers of the astrological clock of Besançon ," I say.

"That is true, the restless spirit of the original clock maker, Monsieur Constant Flavier Bernardin cannot rest in peace because his creation was replaced by another clock built by Monsieur Auguste Lucien Verite. While I was the Besançon astrological clock keeper, I was able to keep them under control as long as I was watching the clock. I don't know what's happened since then," the former Temperatore says.

"We visited the Besançon clock and the rumor is that both clock makers' spirits continue fighting each other and wreaking havoc in the clock tower," I say.

"I've heard about it, but I am done with those two. I simply got tired of their endless fights," he says.

"As I said earlier, we have a proposition for you," I say. "And that will be?" Monsieur Brandibas says.

"We want you to help us persuade both of them to fix the astrological clock of Lyon," Firee says.

"The two of them together? That will never happen," he says totally incredulous.

"The resulting work of repairing and restoring would be credited to both," I say and it immediately catches his attention.

"And that could be a way for both to make peace," Monsieur Brandibas continues thinking aloud and complementing my thought process, "Not a bad idea," he says.

With him tagging along, we use the portal across the street from L'Opera to go back to the L'arc D'Triumph then use its portal for the 2nd and 3rd time to take the Temperatore to talk to each of the contentious clock makers. After long conversations, the clock makers reluctantly agree and along with their tools they join us. Then with trepidation but excited we use the L'arc D'Triumph's portal for the fourth and last time. Our destination is the astrological clock of Lyon. Once on location the two warring watchmakers become fascinated with the watch and we see them soon working together to solve the mechanical problem the clock has. They work incessantly until they fix and put it to work for the enjoyment of the city of Lyon, its people and the visitors from all over the world that come to admire it every year. The moment the clock starts ticking we are back at the L'arc D'Triumph and the giant portal at its center has disappeared.

We are still reeling about the events when we see a glowing door on one of the side walls of the monument. We open it and find a set of lit stairs, we climb them with impetus sensing what's in store for us. At the top of the L'arc D'Triumph we are regaled with a magnificent view of the city of light. We are so mesmerized with the views that we don't notice the arrival of the tall Nordic looking beautiful woman.

"Welcome young wizards," she says from our backs.

Excited we turn around and there she is, our trusted mentor and book antiquarian with long golden braids in a ponytail, Lettizia Dilletante.

"You've all been doing a phenomenal job," she says wearing a big wide smile, "c'mon, follow me, there's no time to waste," she says walking into yet another portal.

We follow her and cross it in tandem. On the other side what we find is her traveling store of antique books. It is a 3 story building and its outside sign reads:

"Dilletante and Dilletante Antiquarians"
(est. a century and a half ago)

We walk in and take our usual sitting place right in the center of the store's atrium. Mrs. Dilletante is ready for us.

"Youngsters, I have a reading here for you that will be a great complement to the experience you just had with the Temperatore and the clock makers.

"The Sculptor and the Stone"

First he saw the stone in a dream...
The next day,
his oneiric experience
morphed into a clear and crisp image,
a vividly and sharp artistic visualization.
The genial artisan
demanded the finest of all marbles,
he expected a stone block with no flaws.
The awesome sculptor
wanted the whitest of all colors.
It's purity and perfection to jump at first sight.
Its smoothness and delicacy to be palpable
and immediately responsive
to his experienced craftsman touch.
His exacting orders were carried out many times
over at the famous Carrara quarries in northern Italy.
But none of the blocks
the masterful artist ever received met his expectations
hence they were used for lesser projects.
Then he saw her,
the subject of his work walking down the street
that ran right in front of his iconic workshop
and straight into Florence's city center.
Her skin seemed like delicate porcelain,

her facial features projected innocence,
candor goodness, and joy.
Her hair cascaded all the way to her waistline.
Her shape and curves were gentle, soft, and classic.
Anatomically and artistically speaking,
she was all he ever wanted.
As time passed by,
the talented artist found himself in a quandary.
He had the idea and he had the subject
but he did not have the stone.
Thus, until one good day, running late to mass,
he found the front door of the cathedral already closed;
running to the sides he looked for an opening;
having found one he rushed in,
but as he was climbing the door steps,
he caught a glimpse of it and stopped right in his tracks.
With eyes of prey, transfixed,
he moved in deliberate slow motion;
from afar it was hardly visible,
but up close,
right behind the thin layer of underbrush,
there it was a large marble stone block
with the whitest of all colors.
Underneath the dirt, time passage, and weather traces;
while caressing the stone,
the daring artist was immediately able to feel and touch
the purity and flawlessness of the white marble underneath.
It turned out that the marble stone had been lying
on the side of the cathedral for decades.
Abandoned right after its arrival,
the commissioned sculptor had deemed it
too narrow for any work to be done out of it.
Over time the city and its people had simply forgotten about it.

Weeks later
with city approval, the unwanted rock
was moved to the genial artist's workshop.
Its narrowness to others,
was utter perfection to him.
The masterful sculptor simply saw in it what others didn't.
An even more difficult proposition though
was to find and persuade his intended muse.
So much so,
that before she ever posed for him he had to win her heart over;
Along the way, she conquered his as well.
So the bachelor sculptor and the subject of his artistic desire
ended up marrying each other,
becoming husband and wife.
Sculpting the stone took years;
the passionate artist's chisel carved, chipped
and sandpapered incessantly; over and over again,
every inch of the stone.
It all required precision and accuracy,
any error or mistake was probably irredeemable
and likely irrecoverable.
The stone slowly morphed progressively
into congruent shapes and forms ever more challenging;
Yet the artist did it all with joy.
The flow seemed trivially easy;
From the beginning his visualization
and preparation of the work to be done
enabled his subsequent flawless execution;
Also, knowing exactly the stone he needed
and not accepting anything less or different,
allowed him to sculpt it
with comfort, gusto, and confidence.
What he didn't expect

or had never experienced before, was true love.
Besides,
with his model being the subject of his adoration;
a much higher level of passion
permeated and soaked his talents and execution.
Over five centuries old,
the real life-sized sculpture
has become a timeless masterpiece;
the beauty of the muse's face glows under the sparkle of love.
The delicate skin exudes beauty and perfection;
Her figure under rich clothes can be easily sensed;
Her anatomy stands out for its great detail;
The visible phalanges are all notoriously present;
their silhouettes, posture, and positioning
all seem ergonomically alive.
Immortalized forever, the great sculptor's muse
is a statue symbolizing Love in all its dimensions into eternity.
The sculptor's greatest achievement though,
consisted in not only bringing his genius along;
including preparing, visualizing, and having the right stone;
but while graced with true love as well,
being able to incorporate it in his work;
creating an even higher level of artistic passion,
where the artist achieved the most sublime connection
between Harmony, Perfection, and Love.
And though they stayed together until their passing;
had many children
and he created many other masterpieces;
She only posed for him that once and he never asked her either;
As true love is neither imitable nor replaceable
the sculptor's muse could only be created once, forever more.
The beautiful fable captures our imagination.

We are all seated in awe of the tale when our trusted mentor brings us back to reality.

"Young wizards, you've shown genial skills when solving the riddle of the L'arc D'Triumph's portal then by negotiating with the Temperatore and finally letting him, in turn, handle the clockmakers; as a consequence both worked in tandem to repair the Lyon astrological clock," she says, "Checkered, what link do you see between the sculptor's fable and the repair of the Lyon astrological clock?" she asks.

"They both required great experience," Checkered responded.

"Breezie, what motivated both the sculptor and the watch makers to complete their job?" Mrs. Dilletante asks.

"Passion and inspiration," he replies.

"Reddish, the nine images on the L'arc D'Triumph's portal only afforded you four opportunities to use it. This posed a totally different type of riddle for you to solve, what do you think was the key for you to solve it?" she asks.

"First of all Firee's rational mind. His logic got us started. Also, the lessons we had just learned about how to deal with uncertainty and making choices," she says.

"Greenie, you learned the power of sensing danger after your performance in the Sorbonne, but you did not use that power on this occasion, why?" Mrs. Dilletante asks.

"Yes we did. Thanks to it, we were pretty much aware that there was nothing threatening us at any instance of the L'arc D'Triumph's portal riddle. Hence we never had to revert to being invisible nor did we have to communicate through thoughts only," she replies.

"Blunt, why the images of the three men on the L'arc D'Triumph's portal could not be something other than the Temperatore and the two clockmakers of the Besançon astrological clock?" the book antiquarian asks.

"When we first faced the images of the six clocks we knew and the images of three men we didn't, the first conclusion we made was that those three images were linked somehow with the clocks. The second conclusion was that the only threesome described to us during those visits to the six clocks was that of the two warring spirits of the clock makers and the Temperatore of the clock of Besançon.

"But how did you guys link them to repairing a totally different clock, in this case the Lyon astrological clock?" Mrs. Dilletante asked.

"That was not a logical deduction like identifying the three men's images, but more of a leap of faith. There was a clock in need of repair.

So, intuitively we inferred that it was their mission to repair it," I say.

"What was it then the common virtue that the six of you, the Temperatore, the clockmakers, the sculptor, and his muse exhibited?" Mrs. Dilletante asks.

Once more we are ready for the key question of the moment and respond in unison:

"Tolerance!"

"Brilliant, just brilliant," Mrs. Dilletante says with a beaming smile on his face, "you are almost there. Do not lower your guard," she says blowing a kiss and vanishing in a hiss.

Her antique books store fades away with her as well. We are all back standing atop the L'arc D'Triumph contemplating a glorious cloudless sky. The gorgeous city view is stunning. As we enjoy the sight panning slowly over the streets, buildings, and gardens we run into the iconic silhouette of our next destination. There it is standing tall Paris' timeless obelisk, the Eiffel Tower; the site of our final six challenges to become master wizards.

Chapter 10

"THE EIFFEL TOWER CHALLENGE"

We descend through the walls of the L'arc D'Triumph to the street level by virtue of our sticky extremities. Out of extreme caution on the way down we decide to go invisible and switch to thought communications only. At street level, we walk along the elegant Avenue Kebler headed to our destination.

Soon our companions join us. Thumbpee as usual on my shoulder and Buggie hovering just above.

"You guys have earned yourselves a new power with high praises from Mrs. Dilletante. From now on you'll be able to use all your powers on your final six challenges," the spec of a man says.

"What about the two of you?" I ask.

"You want us at the Eiffel Tower as well?" Thumbpee asks as Buggie's intense and intermittent buzzes seem to indicate that the flying bug likes the idea very much indeed.

"Ok, hold on a second let me consult father...excuse me, the Orloj," he says and disappears.

Right after Buggie does the same.

We don't need to wait much. In less than a minute, I feel the light bump on my shoulder again.

"The Orloj laughed hard for as long as we were with him," says Thumbpee.

In the meantime Buggie is back as well.

"And what did he say?" asks Breezie.

"That he would have been very disappointed if you had not

asked. So we have his blessing," says the diminutive man.

As we walk further through the regal street we start to sense danger. Soon we start to see them, they are everywhere; translucent creatures on the trees, on the balconies, floating in the air. Hideous figures; gargoyles, witches, one-eyed gold tooth pirates; they all seem to be trying to find us.

'Stop' thinks Breezie dropping an arm across Firee's chest to block his way.

Breezie points at the floor; Firee is within inches of hitting a can of soda. We resume our walk now moving with even greater care, aware of what lies on the floor. We all dread the dangerous sensation building inside all of us. The entire street is filled with menacing forms. It is only when we turn left to face the Eiffel tower that the sense of danger begins to subside. The closer we get the taller the iconic tower seems; the lesser the feeling of danger becomes.

The Challenge of Respect

Once we are at the base of the tower we have a choice to make; do we go up the stairs or on one of the elevators. The decision is not difficult, we decide for the harder of the two and right away start to climb the open-air narrow stairs. A beautiful and sunny day filters through the tower structure. We are surrounded by brown steel bars and huge screws in every direction, shape, and size. The more we climb the more we are encased in metal. That's when we hear the commotion in the distance. The ground's vibration can felt on the metal structure we are standing on. There's an increasing rumble happening not far away. When we are able to focus on the source, we can't believe our eyes. Like a fast-forward movie taking place we see cranes sprout and erected in seconds. Then construction takes place at an amazing speed. At first, we can't distinguish what it is that is being built. There are four structures grouped like a square, going up at the same time; but as they each reach a few stories high, we can see the metal skeleton starting to take shape and look more and more familiar; when a bit higher, the four structures all connect through a single platform, it becomes too obvious.

"A twin Eiffel Tower? Seems like it," I say.

It just takes a few more minutes and a carbon copy of the tower we are in is fully completed standing and glowing all over.

"It is translucent," points out Reddish.

Just above us, we hear a metallic hum. It is continuous; then we see it. Piloting a bicycle seemingly floating in thin air someone is approaching us at high speed.

"Guys look, there is a high wire connecting the two towers, the bicycle is riding over it," points out Breezie, "It's riding the cable on its rims; it has no tires," he adds.

On the bicycle there is a man piloting it; he wears a white bodysuit from head to toe. As it approaches, we can see that the bicycle has two seats and two steering wheels facing opposite ends. The man on the bicycle reaches the tower at the end of the cable and is now parked right in front of us. While holding the tower structure for support with one hand, he seems to notice the six of us and pointing with his finger invites us to get even closer. As we don't sense any danger, we do so. From a small opening in the tower structure we are now inches away from him facing the point where the wire connects with the Eiffel tower.

"Aren't you scared?" asks Greenie to the strange figure with words filled with ingenuity.

"Silly of you Greenie, he is a wizard, how could he be scared?" counters Breezie.

We see the figure making gestures again; first pointing a finger to himself then with the same finger pointing at us and finally pointing at the second seat on the bicycle.

"He seems to be a mute," says Reddish.

"That we don't know. What he is for sure is a mime," Firee says as the acrobat is now all giggles seemingly in agreement with all we are saying.

The mime once more invites us.

"I am not riding that thing, are you crazy?" Greenie snaps at the mime.

Breezie on the other hand takes a step forward and mounts the bike's front seat as the mime holds it firm for him. In a swift move, the mime takes the back seat and starts to pedal; Breezie reacts and does the same in a hurried and clumsy way. The last facial gesture we see from Breezie is one of panic along with a prolonged scream. Then the unexpected happens, the mime jumps off the bike and lands in perfect balance on the wire leaving Breezie alone pedaling away. After a short while, we see Breezie peeking to the back and along with it the bike swaying to the side. Breezie's athleticism kicks in and instinctively he picks up speed and straightens the bike. The mime in the meantime walks behind Breezie losing more and more distance as they move along. We in the meantime are all on edge.

'Breezie remember that you can hover,' I think for him and everyone to hear.

'But only one of us can hover at any one time,' Firee reminds us.

'Thanks Blunt. I've never been so scared in my life,' Breezie thinks as we see him reach the other end of the cable on the translucent version of the Eiffel Tower.

'You have done it without our power to hover,' points out Greenie.

'I actually did, but I wouldn't recommend it to anyone,' Breezie replies.

Soon after, we see the mime reach the other end of the wire as well. Breezie disembarks and the mime zooms right back on the bike. Once again when he reaches us, he makes the same invitation. Every one of us hesitates.

"Checkered c'mon, ride with me. If needed I'll hover and carry you," I say aloud pressing her. Her facial expression of total fear subsides.

This time the mime simply pushes us from behind as we begin to pedal. What we have not realized beforehand is that the wire does swing slightly up and down and to the sides. We feel as if we are about to fall and only the bike speed we maintain by pedaling hard prevents it from happening. We remain rigid as if any tiny movement or lean will make us lose balance. 'Don't look down, left or right. Stay focused only on the way forward,' I think for Checkered to hear.

When we make it to the other end, I firmly take a hold of a rail from the translucent tower. Releasing all her tension at once Checkered sticks her nail in my arm and starts to shake. Breezie and I help her dismount the bike and into the translucent tower. Before we notice the mime has arrived walking the wire and has departed once more on the bike. Caught by surprise we don't notice Breezie leaving us hovering until he gently reaches the moving bike and sits behind the mime who by his body movements is totally shocked.

'He went to pick up the girls,' I point out.

But I am only partially right, he actually does three round trips as our non-athletic genius Firee also needs to be hand-held and crossed as well.

Once we all are safely across we proceed to climb more of the translucent structure, but we don't climb much as the sight to our left side totally captures our imagination. The inside of the translucent tower is a hollow structure that creates a massive atrium. The place is all lit up and filled with trapezes and acrobats swinging then jumping in the air and landing in some cases by gripping both hands on the trapezes' bars and others by being grabbed in the air by other acrobats. It happens so fast that we don't have time to react; a trapezist swings all the way towards us, he is held to the trapeze by his legs wrapped around two cables and the bar, he reaches his maximum altitude inches from us at eye level. Then in the brief moment that he pauses before falling back, he grabs both of Greenie's hands and takes her with him. We hear her scream and see in horror as she swings to the other side and on the way up is thrown in the air. We see her flying as a cannon ball then as she begins to fall another pair of hands grab's Greenie's and takes her with him. I am about to send her a thought to hover when also out of the blue another trapezist grabs Reddish's arms and swings down and away with her. Fractions of a second later Checkered is gone as well, followed by Firee. Surprisingly, to Breezie and I the only thing delivered to us are a couple of trapezes' bars. As we are thinking what to do, the mime pushes us from behind and all of the sudden we are in the air gripping the bars for dear life while swinging with the trapeze. On the way down I already know that I don't have the strength to hold the grip for long, So when I reach the bottom of the swing I let go of the grip and begin to fall. But no sooner I am loose I begin to hover. At that moment Breezie zooms past me on his way down, having lost his grip of the bar as well. I chase and catch him in time to halt his fall, then I immediately deposit his shocked self on one of the side platforms. I hover up and pick up my mates one by one from their swinging trapezes and gather them all with Breezie. My rescue mission completed I finally land myself next to them. To our great surprise, another acrobat lands next to us, trapeze on hand. He extends a hand for Reddish to join him. A second one quickly arrives and invites Greenie. Then a third does the same with Checkered. This is a crucial moment in our challenge. Giving them comfort when they all look at me, I nod my head giving them consent. Surprisingly none of the three hesitates and are gone in an instant. Next, Breezie, Firee and myself have three acrobats handing trapezes to each one of us as well. This time they strap our wrists to the trapeze bars. Next, we are all swinging away. The six of us now fly the translucent tower's atrium space having fun. I see Greenie, Reddish and Checkered having a blast while being thrown in the air between trapezists. They are laughing and enjoying as my two mates Breezie and Firee and myself do as well.

Once we have all been returned safely to the platform, our Iberian mate opens the conversation.

"I didn't see any danger coming, what about you guys?" asks an excited Reddish, "On either occasion," she adds.

"The reason is because there was no real danger," I say and immediately grab everyone's attention, "This is after all a challenge," I add.

"That is absolutely true, dear Blunt," says our mentor and book antiquarian Cornelious Tetragor, "Congratulations young wizards, you have succeeded in overcoming the challenge of respect," he says and after a slight bow of the head, he vanishes.

"He was short in words," observes Breezie.

"Tetragor wants to keep it formal so we stay focused and do not become over-confident," I say.

"And now what do we do?" asks Greenie, "Ah...I know...Thumbpee, Buggie can you guys show yourselves," she says giggling.

The Challenge of Indifference

"There they are, our trusted guides or shall we say, now our companions; for the first time on one of our challenges," says Greenie.

"I've got two things to say. The evil forces of the dark and occult arts cannot reach you while you are in the virtual Eiffel Tower. Pay close attention to one of your readings with Mr. Kraus, not everything is what it seems and not everyone means what they say," the spec of a man says while as customary sitting on my shoulder.

"Thumbpee, which of the two towers are we supposed to climb?" asks Checkered.

"Your question surprises me, isn't that already obvious to you?" the minuscule man replies and vanishes in disgust.

"Both, Checkered, Both," Firee says.

"How do you know?" she presses obfuscated.

"Why are we in any of them but for that purpose?" Firee argues closing the subject.

Flustered, Checkered turns away to look at the acrobatics taking place across the atrium. That's when she notices it, "Guys, look all the way up," we all do. At the very top of the tower from the angle we are looking from, seems to be the floor of the top of the tower. Right there we see two bright letters shining in Vegas fashion: "L & L".

"What would that be? What is the meaning of those two letters?" Greenie asks.

"We may as well go and find out," Breeze replies and starts to climb the stairs.

We all follow climbing the open-air narrow stairs of the translucent tower. There is only one problem, the stairs suddenly become an escalator that is activated on a descending mode only. And the faster we climb, the faster the escalator's steps descend. Breezie leads the way with his athletic instincts and takes over; as he climbs he explores the handrail to see if it's easier to walk up over it. No can do. It's also moving downwards at the same speed. Then we see him trying to hover. He can't! The ceiling has closed on us, then we see him looking for space between the rail and the translucent steel structure. There is no space! In the meantime we continue to be stuck without gaining any ground against the rapidly descending steps. Next, Breezie slows down until he reaches a pace that though quite fast is perhaps only 3/4 of the way of the fastest speed he has tried so far. We all follow his pace. At that pace, we all notice that though with great effort we start to make progress climbing. By increasing it a notch, Breezie fine-tunes the pace a bit more. Now we climb steadily in slow motion while our legs still continue to move extremely fast against a cascade of downward moving steps. It takes us quite a while to reach the top. We are all perspiring and out of breath when we have the top platform within our reach. Then the unexpected happens and it catches us all off-guard. In a snap all the steps drop and fold flat, making the surface of the escalator into a greasy slide. Lying flat on our butt we begin to descend at high-speed. We try to grip the handrails. Fruitless they are full of grease. After countless twists and turns, we make it all the way down to our original starting point. Frustrated, we stand on the platform and glance at the rooftop as far away as we were a while ago. Unexpectedly, the mime is back and he is pointing to six parallel zip lines right in front of us. The cables go all the way down to the translucent tower's atrium ground floor.

"He is asking us to go down when we need to go up?" says Greenie aloud.

But the moment she says it, the words sound familiar and take all of us back to Prague and the introductory reading each one of us had with Mr. Kraus.

"An upside-down world," I say.

"To go up you actually have..."I begin to say and we all complete the sentence "...you have to go down and vice-versa."

The mime straps each one of us to the zip lines but does not let anyone go until we are all ready. Then he signals for us to start zipping down the line. The moment we start, the most amazing thing happens. Defying the laws of gravity our entire surroundings start to rotate around the zip line's axis, it happens as we gather more and more speed. Our destination has inverted! Instead of the ground floor now the new bottom is the top of the tower. For the purpose of our zip line trek, the tower has gone upside down. When we reach our destination, the mime is waiting for us. He does not let us get off but ties our harnesses lines to the platform floor first. He then gives us the thumbs up and we all begin to step into our destination. But before we touch the ground, our surroundings rotate 180 degrees in a snap. Now we are dangling from the lines attached to the platform. The tower has reverted to its natural position. It is no longer upside down. The mime then pulls us up one by one into the steel platform. The gigantic sign: "L & L" is atop of our heads. We find a set of narrow steps on the side and filled with curiosity we climb them. We don't know that we are in for the surprise of our lives. At the end of the stairs, we reach the very top of the tower. It is an enclosed room of glass and steel. It is gloriously filled with Louis XV furniture and ornaments. In the center of the room, there are two very similar-looking young men with dashing Clark Gable and Alain Delon looks. One is dressed in full military regalia; medals, ribbons, and all. The other one is dressed in sharp contrast as a pirate, though a neatly pressed and seemingly wealthy one indeed.

"Welcome young wizards, my name is Lafayette, Marquis De La Fayette," says the military man.

"Pleased to meet you, my name is Lafitte."

'Guys for those of you that don't know it, for some time these two were the most famous Frenchmen in the Americas," I think for everyone to hear.

"You are right, Blunt," says LaFayette reading my mind, "I assisted and fought for the Americans including Gen. Washington on their war of independence against England," he adds.

"And I wreaked havoc in the Caribbean; smuggling anything of high-profit as well as capturing any wealth that crossed our sights," says Lafitte.

"A freedom fighter and a pirate at the same time, each a legend in their own right," says Firee.

"Well it is time for you to experience first-hand what we did," says LaFayette.

"And why in final analysis we were two sides of the same coin," adds Lafitte.

A floor-to-ceiling display slides open like a curtain covering an entire wall of the room. To our amazement as the images start, both our hosts simply walk into it, and right after the imagery begins and it immediately enraptures us in such a way that we feel as if we are present at the events that are taking place. The narration that follows clearly explains it all for us.

"Lafitte versus Lafayette"

Deep in the bayou in the Louisiana swamps,
the ragged band of outlaws,
Buccaneers in the land and the seas, download the riches,
they took just a few days ago from a Spanish armada
they decimated to nothing in a bloody battle of the seas.
Their leader, dashing Monsieur Lafitte
is a sort of Robin Hood taking from some hoarding
more than they need,
and giving to many others that truly have a use for it.
Tonight their cache of stolen weapons
is changing hands for nothing;
along the muddy and still waters,
wooden box after wooden box,
moves through a human chain,
ammunition, muskets, and pistols they contain.
The insurgent smile for the timely receipt of basic supplies
from such an unlikely source as Lafitte is a buccaneer,
a swash-buckling outlaw,
that takes from empires in decline
and gives to those building a new one,

those freedom fighters
fighting to form a mighty country,
The United States of America.
Along the shores of the Delaware River,
the powerful French Navy flotilla lies in wait
in the middle of the night.
The idea and planning for the daring mission
has been instigated by a brave visionary
and dashing young French military man;
a profound "connoisseur"
of the affairs of the English colonies
and a close collaborator of General George Washington,
including his independence movement
to free up the colonies
from the British crown.
Once the French navy meets the rebels,
wooden box after wooden box, moves through a human chain
ammunition, muskets, and pistols they contain.
The insurgents smile for the timely receipt of basic supplies
from such an unlikely source,
a swash-buckling French man,
The Marquis De LaFayette,
an officer from another country's army,
who has convinced his own government
to give General Washington's freedom fighters' troops,
the much-needed armament as they fight
to form a mighty country, The United States of America.

"Exactly as they said. Two sides of the same coin," I reflect.

As we part ways with the brave twosome in unison as a sign of profound respect we all bow our heads to the unlikely duo for allowing us to take a peak into the American war of Independence.

We are back to a now empty platform atop the translucent tower. Waiting for us with a huge smile is no other than our book antiquarian and mentor, Lazarus Zeetrikus.

"Well done young wizards. I am very proud of you. You've just demonstrated mastery on the vice of indifference. A few more challenges and you are done. But pay attention they will be hard throughout," he says as he tips his hat and vanishes in an instant.

Thumbpee and Buggie are back. This time we don't need to call them for a change.

"You have all walked through fire and ice. Now you'll have to learn to walk on air...Ah! before I forget. As the laws of physics do not exist in such space, none of you will be able to hover in between the towers; the magnetic field that spreads between the two towers will knock you down. Finally, the next challenge will have two separate occurrences, and your will have to overcome both," says Thumbpee before vanishing again.

Buggie exits the room into the open air and points down with his tiny green laser beam. The tiny ray goes all the way down to the base of the tower. Then with his intense buzz, Buggie flies away at high speed.

The Challenge of Selflessness

We don't understand what Thumbpee's clue means, so our first instinct is to take the stairs down, but when Greenie heads to the corner of the room, the entrance to the stairs is no longer there. Breezie gets it before we all do, so he does not waste any time and climbs out. We all peek outside and see him extending a leg out trying to find footing in the air! To his and our surprise he quickly finds it to his right. Now seating on the ledge he probes with both feet together and realizes that the invisible surface in front of him is wide enough for both feet; in a continuous movement he stands and is now literally standing in the air! Next,

Breezie carefully opens his stance until he reaches the edges on both sides of the invisible step. He then carefully probes the front and back edges. His movements give us an idea of the size of the landing, about a foot long by about a foot wide. Breezie now sits on the invisible step with legs again dangling from the edge again. Right in front of him, though a bit lower, he reaches another step with the tip of his shoe.

"Try to see if there is a handrail, Breezie," I say.

He now stands on the invisible step and seems more confident. With his hands, he probes the air at his waist level and sure enough he finds it. We all see the expression of happiness on his face. now with decisiveness, while holding the invisible handrail, he takes his first step, then a second; the handrail serves as his guide both for direction and the downward slope. From our perspective we see Breezie walking through the air, descending gently in a serpent-like trajectory. But we are in for another surprise when I take the second turn for safety. At the very last second, a gut feeling prevents me from taking the first step standing where Breezie started. As Breezie did, I sit and dangle my legs from the edge of the two-tier rooftop. Now I can appreciate the abyss in front of me as vertigo creeps through my veins. From the corner of my eye, even If I don't want to, I can see all the way down to the base of both towers. But there is no first step. Instinctively I start to slide to the side of the ledge and continue probing with my feet until a couple of feet to my left, I find my first step.

'Guys, each one of us has its own set of steps. Each of you gently sit down on the edge of the roof and imitate Breezie and me.' I think for everyone to hear.

In the meantime I stand up on the first landing as he did. Next, I find the handrail and start my way down, seemingly walking in the air as well. Soon, the six of us are zigzagging our way down. That's when suddenly we see Breezie hanging from the handrails.

Quickly, he swings himself back to the precedent step.

'My stairway ends here,' he thinks for all of us to hear.

The problem is that he is only halfway down and we are a bit behind. Everyone stops out of an abundance of caution and is none us is any longer confident about each of our individual paths.

'Now that I think about it, we've all been holding the stairs left handrail,' points out Firee.

'Is there a right side handrail?' asks Greenie.

'I don't know. But we may as well find out,' thinks Breezie.

Sliding across the invisible step it takes no time for him to find it on the other end. Now holding the right side handrail, he immediately starts to climb back up. About twenty steps later he finds an interruption on the handrail; right away he probes with his feet and we can all see that he has found a landing at the same level. Next, we see him walking into it looking once more for a handrail, but he can't find one.

'Guys, I am losing grip on my stance,' 'Breezie, but you are standing," I think.

But then we see how Breezie's feet slowly spread out until he falls flat on his butt and starts what appears to be a slide floating through the air. He is zigzagging sideways through the air descending through an invisible slide that does not seem to have much inclination. But that's about to change, picking up speed as the invisible slide dips; in rapid succession, he takes a sharp turn to the right then one to the left, we hear his first scream when he takes a jump upwards and drops hard, it is followed by a jump downwards with a harder landing; now at a much higher speed he is propelled up like a cannonball. He raises almost all the way back to our level then yelling non-stop he drops into a free-fall all the way down. Right next to the ground, he hits some sort of invisible net that slows him down until we see him stepping out of whatever held him onto the ground. The remainder of us, one by one follow the right handrail down until the interruption. Then with mixed emotions walk the plank and plunge down in equally spectacular fashion.

Soon we are all back at the base of the original Eiffel Tower. That's when we hear the familiar grumbling for a second time. Once again the rumbling and tremor is followed by cranes, but the fast-forward movie this time is in reverse motion. The tower starts to unbuild itself from top to bottom. In a few minutes, the rapidly decreasing translucent tower copy reaches ground level, then the cranes disappear and the lush and green grounds behind the Eiffel Tower are back to their splendorous selves.

No sooner are we out of the initial shock, the first one to react is Reddish. She runs and hugs Breezie, the rest of us soon follow and it quickly turns into a pile on. We even, albeit briefly, lift him off the ground as this challenge's hero. To cap it all he receives several kisses on the cheeks from the three girls.

Thumbpee and Buggie only make a brief appearance and are quickly gone.

"On the second part of this challenge your portal power will not work," is the only thing the spec of a man says before vanishing in an instant.

Feeling relaxed we walk for a second time to the tower's entrance. Strangely enough, all the tower's stairs, points of access are closed; the only choices are the elevators. Without thinking too much about it, we board one of the elevators and select the first level. It is when the doors close with a bang that the sense of danger hits us all. Too late. The elevator rockets up at such speed that our face's skin stretches out as if made out of plaster. Our screams and yells are deafened by the roar of the elevator going at high speed through its metallic rails. We all lower ourselves to seating positions tightly bundled against one another on the floor. The elevator starts to brake hard, so much that it feels like it's going to break apart. The floor lights indicate that we have reached the top. But there is no time for comfort. The elevator hops twice then precipitates into a free- fall; dropping at a vertiginous speed we hold unto each other as tightly as we can. The strong sense of danger throws me into a total state of emergency. I try to think but the gravity forces are crushing my whole self. The floor lights have us dropping past halfway. Then it hits me, 'there is no good outcome, we have to save ourselves,' I think, 'shield!,' Breezie thinks.

We are all seated against the floor when the dome shield covers us. 'Hover,' I think.

Next I hover up into the ceiling of the dome. Then pushed by my hovering efforts, the dome starts to float up in the elevator's cabin and it almost reaches the ceiling. We are now shielded from some of the g-forces of the fall. Then with tremendous force, we hit the ground at maximum speed. The elevator's floor is crushed upwards towards us. We brace for impact but it stops right short of us. The walls are all bent as well but by us floating, no surface makes any impact with us. Between the six of us, we pull the elevator doors open and step out. The first face we see standing and waiting for is that of our grandmotherly book antiquarian and mentor, Lucrecia van Egmond.

"Congratulations dear youngsters, you have overcome, although with difficulties, the challenge of selflessness," she says with a broad smile while hugging us one by one, "The last one was a trap right?" asks Greenie. "It sure was, by no other than your old nemesis, the dwarf. It only took a tiny lapse in concentration from you all, forgetting that the evil forces do operate in the original tower. You did not pause to ask yourselves why the stairs were closed. Also, you entered the elevator so quickly that you only felt the sense of danger when it was too late and you were already inside. Nevertheless, somehow you found a brilliant solution to overcome what most certainly would have ended your quest. Besides, your execution of the invisible steps challenge as a team and Breezie's selflessness was superb. Keepyour guards up though," Mrs. van Egmond says before bowing out and disappearing in an instant.

Shaken and stirred we look at each other with scolding gestures. No one is happy with the elevator incident.

"Isn't it ironic, we've completed three challenges so far, but we are still at the base of the Eiffel Tower," says Reddish sarcastically breaking the collective foul mood we are all in.

We turn around to begin our climb and to our surprise the elevators are in pristine condition and naturally, the stairs are all open.

'Guys, let's go into invisible mode and thought communications only,' I think for everyone to hear it.

The Challenge of Deafness

We climb the stairs with our eyes wide open. After a steady climb for what seems a long time, once again we are nicely above the city of light on a glorious sunny day. Around a tight bend we run into a restaurant. At least that's what the exterior signs says. We walk and find a story-high open hall made out of steel and glass. What awaits us is everything but a place to eat French gourmet food. In front of us there are six electricity rings standing vertically, as if they were portals, the rings are thin yet large in size, about eight feet tall by six feet wide. Their sparks seem alive and wild, highly visible and intimidatingly noisy. The intensely bright rings are organized in a circle about six feet apart from each other. We are all mesmerized by the sight. We are not surprised when our expert in physics takes the first step. As if hypnotized, Firee walks towards the closest ring. Once in front, he tries to extend his arm through the center of the ring but before crossing the ring, it's rejected with a spark and an obvious electrical discharge judging by Firee's reaction in pain. Yet, he does not quit; we see him walking outside the circle and walking into the next ring. This time his arm barely peeks into the ring before it gets bounced out albeit this time with less intensity. The same thing happens on his third intent; it is on his fourth ring try when his hand finally crosses the circle.

'Guys this is my circle, 'he thinks turning back to us with a big wide smile. One by one we start to try the other five sparking rings. Reddish and Breezy find their rings but Greenie, Checkered, and I try each of the three remaining rings but are rejected by all, once again we are all baffled... except Firee. His logical mind is not deterred easily.

"Greenie, try Breezie's ring," he says but she's rejected as well, "Come over, try mine," he says and this time it works.

Checkered tries my ring and it works and Reddish is successful with Breezie's as well.

"Pairs guys, we've been set up as pairs," Firee says.

"But we are only using three of the rings, "states Greenie with her usual exuberance.

"There must be a good reason for it, I'll bet you that we will be using the other three rings as well," Firee says setting the stage.

"Time to go in then," he says and we all cross the rings in tandem.

Once on the other side Checkered and I are on an empty white room. Its brightness briefly blindsides us until we adjust. The floor, walls and low ceiling are made out of small square panels. Their color is generated by back lights. While Checkered and I are standing together, a panel to her right turns red for a fraction of a second, then just above me, one panel turns green for a brief moment. Next in rapid succession, multiple panels light up in different colors. Soon we are bombarded with flashes of color from all of the room panels. Then it stops and all the room turns white again; neither Checkered nor myself have figured things out yet.

Suddenly the flashing begins again but this time, at least at first we are able to follow the sequence; a panel to her right turns red, the one on the top turns green; one by one the panels light up until the pace accelerates beyond a discernible path that either of us can follow, the sequence continues until the same finale with all panels flashing in different colors until it stops.

"Did you notice there is a pause between the one-by-one panel flashing sequence and the pace picking up uncontrollably?" I say.

"Come to think of it yes, but what is the meaning of it?" she asks.

"Perhaps something we should memorize?" I think aloud.

"And the moment to do it is on that pause?" she says.

And that's what we do. During the brief pause Checkered presses the red panel and I do the green; we continue until we successfully complete the ten-panel sequence before it runs wild. The moment we do, the entire room flashes back and forth as if congratulating us. So we have to do it before the panels run wild," I say.

We notice that one panel on the opposite end has become translucent.

"That's our reward; we have to earn enough of them to get out," I say.

Then it becomes more difficult. Now, the sequence is not only different but every single panel flashes in quick succession and sometimes only once; others twice even three times in random fashion. The sequence is also longer. Right after the panel lights have run amok again I wonder aloud, "I'm not sure I've memorized the sequence yet, what about you?"

"Almost all of it, do you want to try?" Checkered asks.

"Alright then, nothing to lose," I say.

Once we reach the pause we give it a try. Checkered presses twice a red panel and I press once a yellow one; she then does thrice a purple one; hesitating ever so briefly I press once a black one and realize a tad too late that I should have pressed it twice; suddenly the entire room goes dark followed by a deafening and chirring sound; next we are back to an all-white room. But the room not only has become significantly smaller, the lone transparent panel has turned white again! We are back to square one. Almost without pause, the room's panel starts flashing the first sequence once again. And we clear it with ease. On our second panel flashing sequence, we are more careful ensuring we have memorized the sequence well before we attempt to press the panels with the same sequential order. Our memory and retention abilities have expanded a great deal. Once we have enough transparent panels. They have formed into the shape of a door and the flashes have stopped altogether. But when we try to cross them it's not possible. Each one of us tries then both together, no can do. Then the room goes black again. What happens next is at first incomprehensible then fascinating; we first notice them as tiny points of light in the floor and ceiling. Simultaneously and in slow motion; thin laser beams in multiple colors, start to drop from the ceiling and others rise from the floor. We now have countless laser beams blocking the way between us and the translucent door. Checkered tries to touch one of the beams with the tip of her finger but immediately withdraws it, "it's burning hot," she says. I try another one and the same thing happens. Nevertheless recalling Firee's approach, I go ahead and touch a few more and get scalded each time; this until on my fourth try and a blue laser beam is utterly cold. Checkered's eyes shine in amazement when it happens; I grip it and try to move it forward. Nothing. Backwards, sideways, neither. But when I try to rotate it, it moves! I then rotate the laser beam 45 degrees until is in the 9am in one end and 3pm position in the other end in front of us. When that happens we hear something unlock but it is not visible to us. Intuitively I prompt

Checkered, "Try it again." She does and on her first try is able to grip a yellow laser beam. Yet when she tries to rotate it, she can't. It is on her last move that she can slide the laser beam to the left until it locks. Once again we hear the sound of something unlocking but cannot see it.

"Blunt, look at the bottom half of the translucent door," she says.

I turn around and realize what the unlocking sounds are about; the translucent door is lifting up by steps. Half of it is open already! It is my turn and after guessing the sequence right I slide my laser to the right until it locks. After unlocking sounds, our door is now three-quarters of the way up. Checkered's laser rotates 45 degrees before it locks up. The last unlocking mechanism opens our door all the way. Then, all other laser beams retreat and hide either in the roof or on the floor. In a hurry, we head towards the door but before our second step I grip Checkered's arm and we stop. The four laser beams we have been able to move have formed a perfect square that lies just in front of us.

"Checkered this is the door," I say.

"How do you know?" she asks.

"We have a choice, which one do we take, the obvious one?" I ask.

"I see your point. Is there a way to be sure?" she presses me.

I turn around and throw my watch in the air towards the door. What happens next stuns us. The clock crashes and burns upon contact with the translucent door.

"Blunt, look!" Checkered points out.

The laser beams of the square structure is blurring and starting to fade away. "Jump!" We both plunge into the square as if jumping into a pool. Coincidentally, our experience in school gymnastics serves us well as we are able to roll when landing on the floor. We are back in the Empty Eiffel Tower restaurant hall.

We are lying between two actively and sparking electrical rings. I turn around and see Breezie ad Reddish lying on the floor; also in between two other rings. At that moment we see Firee and Greenie flying out simultaneously from another ring. Their landing is not as elegant as ours though Firee lands flat on his chest and Greenie literally on her butt.

We look at each other as if from worlds apart which in a way we are. Slowly we all come back to reality and knowing there is no time loose.

Each pair of us heads to its adjacent ring. I try with my hand first and it goes safely through. Checkered does the same and has no problem either. We then walk together into our second sparking ring. The room we walk into is built entirely out of steel and glass. It has a magnificent view of Paris. It's all furnished with mahogany and leather, brass and plaid fabrics. On one side of a conference table, there are four men animatedly arguing with one another. On the other side of the table there are two big leather chairs. Checkered and I take a seat not knowing exactly what to expect. The sounds in the room are all crisp. We can hear even hear a pin drop. The acoustics are of absolute high-fidelity. The moment we are seated the men notice us and turn their arguments to us. We hear their words at full blast but can't understand a word they are saying.

"Excuse me gentlemen, we can't understand a word you are saying," I say.

The four men totally ignore my words and continue to talk non-stop.

"Can't you hear us? Your words don't make sense," says Checkered.

Without even flinching the four men continue to talk to us and argue among themselves, their faces show all kinds of expressions that range from anger to being flustered, laughter, mockery, serious.

"Can you at least slow down and turn your volume down?" I say.

Our words are totally ignored while they continue to talk looking down at us straight in the eye.

'Should we stand up and leave,' I think for Checkered to hear.

'I am not sure that giving up on establishing contact is what is expected of us,' she answers.

'They know we are here,' I ponder.

'Right,' Checkered replies.

'But they don't seem to care hearing our words,' I think.

'Let me try something,' Checkered thinks.

She gestures with her hands. First, she points to her chest, then her mouth, then points out to them, finally she points to her ears and signals now moving her pointy finger from side to side.

The four men observe her with bemused faces but the moment she is done, they continue exactly where they left off, arguing among themselves and talking to Checkered and I while looking at us straight in the eye.

'They don't seem to be listening,' I think.

"Gentlemen, we are going to be leaving,' I say but something is wrong.

I can't hear myself. I turn to Checkered.

'I can't hear myself,' I think for her to hear.

'I saw you moving your lips but couldn't hear what you said either,' she replies.

'Try it yourself,' I mull.

I see her address the men and how they ignore her but I can't hear her either. Then it dawns on me.

'Talk to me Checkered,' I think.

'Like this, instead of thinking,' she asks as we both realize that we can hear each other without any problem. But what takes us by surprise is that the four men have stopped talking and are looking at us.

'They heard and paid attention the moment we talked to each other,' I think.

"Why do you think these gentlemen only seem to listen and pay attention to us when we talk to each other? she says aloud emphasizing every word for the foursome to hear.

"Young wizards, in effect you broke the spell the moment you started talking to each other. You see now how others feel when you only listen to yourself in life. You also experienced the panicky feeling when all of a sudden you can't hear your own self. Not nice either right? Finally, you also learned what's the best antidote against those that don't listen. Ignore them and talk to others that do listen to you. You saw how the four of us couldn't stand it and in an instant started listening to you."

The four men then resume their endless argument and discussion. I see that the opposite door of the panoramic conference room has opened. I take Checkered's hand and we walk out with an invaluable lesson.

While stepping out we cross the sparkling electrical ring. We are back in the Eiffel Tower high ceiling restaurant hall. Standing in front of one of the electrified rings are Reddish and Breezie and in front of another are Firee and Greenie. Then all of the sudden, as if a slowly melting ice cream, the six sparking rings vanish. In their place we see our trusted books antiquarian mentor, Paulina Tetrikus, her pretty face shining with joy.

"Young wizards I am proud to congratulate you on overcoming the very trying challenge of deafness. I couldn't be prouder of each one of you," she says before bowing and vanishing in an instant.

The magnificent hall we are in suddenly feels eerie absent of all the action and tension we were experiencing.

"The Challenge of Arrogance"

We exit the hall still reeling about what turned out to be very similar experiences for each of the three twosomes. The iron-made narrow stairs awaits us. Not sensing danger we continue climbing the tower, there are no walls but only the tower structure. So we are exposed to Paris' daytime glorious weather.

"Aren't you letting your guard down once again?" asks Thumbpee who has just turned up on my shoulder.

Buggie's intense yet intermittent buzz not only marks his return but seems to be scolding us as well in still intermittent bursts.

"We failed to go invisible or use thoughts to communica..." this is the last word I try to complete "...Ahhh!"

The step underneath has just vanished and I am in a free fall inside of a black tube. My teeth are clenched, arms tightly pressed against my body; due to the force of the wind, I can feel the skin stretching across my face. I careen from side to side, each slight bump hurts and burns, the air pressure against my eyes is unbearable as if trying to tear them wide open. I start to lose conscience when the tube starts to turn; I hit the opposite end of its cylindrical walls and this time bounce harder back. Next, the curvature of the tube becomes more pronounced as does my bouncing from side to side. When the tube's turn ends, I am propelled upwards at a vertiginous speed; the light of the day comes to me at high- speed and soon after I am shot out of the tube like a cannonball. I fly with my legs up and my arms tightly pressed against my body like an arrow. I go ten, twenty, thirty stories high until I lose momentum and fall precipitously down. Now there is no symmetric shape to my humanity. I drop like a piece of ragged cloth, twisting and turning, unable to cut through the void in any kind of aerodynamic position. At full speed three-quarters of the way down, I hit a massive net. With my face and body pressed against the massive net, I see firsthand, the hidden force of momentum stretching the net towards the street level; the ground is approaching closer and closer until, within a few feet, the net ricochets me back at full speed into the air, this time my flight is shorter. I end up bouncing half a dozen times more until the net levels off. That's when I see my other mates lying around other parts of the net. I realize that the giant net is attached to two corners of the tower on our side and a couple of thick steel columns on the garden grounds where the translucent tower stood.

"Wasn't that awesome?" says Breezie.

"Yeah," exclaims Greenie.

"Before we continue celebrating we may as well get out of here asap," I say.

Using our sticky extremities we crawl back in the direction of the tower. As we get close, the net becomes loose from the two columns, we drop with the net until we are hanging from the side of the net, still attached to the tower.

'Climb guys! Climb' I think aloud.

Like spiders we scud up, and just at the moment when we jump into the tower's open-air stairs, the net detaches from the tower and drops all the way down and hits the ground with a massive thump. In the meantime we are back to the very same spot where our free-fall through the black hole started.

'Let's go invisible, right now,' I think for everyone to hear. In an instant we become transparent.

'Young wizards, this is the second time during the course of the tower's six challenges that you've lost focus and concentration,' says Thumbpee on an ever so brief visit.

'Let's continue up, guys,' I think while I wink and smile at all others. Fact is, danger or no danger, we've just had a blast. Nevertheless, Thumbpee is right and part of our faces reflect expressions of the fun we just had and awareness as well about the seriousness of his message which has been well received.

We climb now with special attention to our power to detect a sense of danger. A couple of stories higher, we run into a second restaurant. The plaque on the wall reads: "Jules Verne Restaurant".

We step in and find a hall with an atrium three-stories high. The tower structure of iron beams, bars, and columns serves along with the panoramic glasses, as the walls of the place. Instead of commensal tables, we see six giant screens with partitions between them. High leather chairs lie in front of each booth. A pair of headphones and virtual reality goggles sit on top of each chair. A magnetic field prevents the wrong person to enter each booth. So we probe until each one of us finds his own spot. I put on the virtual reality goggles and headphones. Right away the 3-D images on my headset make me feel as if I am right in the middle of what is being projected to me.

Me (5 years old), the bicycle anecdote,
Hilton Head Island, S.C.

Wobbly is the best way to describe the five-year-old version of me on a bike. As the sun sets in the horizon, from my booth I am witnessing my parents' attempts to teach me to ride a bike. We are on a beautiful beach with sand as hard as a rock. Countless people ride their bikes close to the water's edge. The island's beach goes on for miles and miles. The only anomaly in the postcard-perfect afternoon is me. My parents try their best to set me up on the right path, one sends me away, the other waits for me on the other end, but I do not follow instructions. So I pretend not to listen to my parents and veer off course and go riding on my own. Mind you that not only do I look clumsy as I pedal, I am also dangerously out of control. The first mishap happens when I lose control and plunge into the water, next is when I run into the empty chairs and coolers of beachgoers, then on the same ride, everything comes to a climax by me crashing head-on with two bikes and knocking down to the sand the elderly couple riding them. As I am being scolded by my parents the image fades away. Then in rapid scenes I see myself on the same bike, pedaling around my mom in Boston, and in succession crashing softly against a tree, recklessly exiting our home's driveway without looking to the sides, followed by a car slamming the brakes inches away from me; next I see myself skidding out of control on our home's entrance and running over several bags of groceries just unloaded by my father from the family's station wagon. Finally, I see myself committing the cardinal sin of bumping my father from the back, making him spill coffee over his treasured briefcase. Virtual reality allows me to experience all of my unruly behavior firsthand. It all leaves me not only embarrassed but also concerned on whether or not now as a teenager I continue to display the same attitude with my parents and others.

I take my goggles and headphones off and immediately see on my five mates the same baffled expressions, realizing that we've just gone through similar experiences.

"Not listening to my parents from such an early an age, made me insufferable ," I say.

"What about me! I truly thought, I knew more than my teachers," says Firee.

"I did not start to listen to my mentor until I was ten years old. I cannot understand how he was able to have so much patience with me while I was ignoring all of his words of wisdom for so long,' says Breezie.

"Self-absorbed preoccupied only about me and social media, it was only recently that I became involved and engaged with others and as a consequence have learned so much from my parents' world of classical music," says Reddish. "Being the leading child sitcom TV actress; being called prodigy made me act during the best part of my childhood like I was superior to others. I mistreated and ignored too many people," says Greenie.

"In my case, I've just witnessed the ridiculous behavior I exhibited, when learning to ride a bike, towards my parents and others. A reckless "know it all" is how I just saw myself in virtual reality," I say.

No sooner I finish, we face a giant screen; on it a scribble starts to scroll...

"She is Everything There Is"

A Noble Mother there is only one,
A Gentle Mother is a treasure we protect
and defend to no end,
A doting Mother is always deserving of all
our honors, love, and respect, each day of our lives,
A giving Mother always does
EVERYTHING AND ANYTHING for us,
something we shall never forget to value and recognize.
Her Maternal Instincts never fail,
Her Maternal Judgements either;
She fiercely defends the good and the bad in us
regardless of circumstances,
She always reads us better than anyone
Correcting and steering us back on track in a snap.
While under her mantle,
No one can feel for us the way she does,
No one can protect us how she does,
Because no one but her carried and nurtured in her womb
that little thing we were,
Before being born.
An Insanely Awesome Mother she always is,
A Blessing, A Godly Gift She deservingly is,
A Noble, Gentle, Doting, Giving, Insanely Awesome Mother,

She Is Everything There Is.

We all look at each other with guilty faces.

"That's precisely what we didn't value enough as we grew up," I reflect aloud.

The moment I finish we hear the clapping.

"Bravo young wizards, bravo. You've just taken full advantage of the challenge of arrogance. Textbook performance, congratulations; you're now so close to becoming master wizards, don't blow it all up now," says our trusted books antiquarian mentor, Morpheous Rubicom just before vanishing into thin air in an instant.

The Challenge of Tolerance

An intense light filters through the restaurant's entrance. Not sensing any danger we head to the door. The blinding brightness originates in the tower's outdoor stairs we've been using. We follow the whiteness up the steps until we reach a bifurcation. To the right, the brown iron tower stairs continue. To the left, we have a shining and wide set of stairs. They are white and head in a sinuous fashion up into the sky and away from the tower. Once again we don't sense any danger so we take them. The moment we step into them and out of the tower we see the sign "stairs to heaven" we start to climb with trepidation. On each side of the handrails, there is a precipice all the way down to the city of light's ground. The temperature drops rapidly and the high-altitude winds pick up. After fifteen minutes of climbing, we start to run into clouds; we climb through the dense fog of seemingly gigantic cloud formations. Paris' blue sky surrounds us; for a moment we are so close to it that it seems as if we could touch it. Finally, we see an immense and uniform set of clouds above us; they cover half of the sky. In the meantime, our bending and undulating set of stairs are leading us into the thick cloud formation. The heavenly stairs take us straight into the thickest of the cloud layer. We continue climbing until we emerge on the other side of it. The cloud layer seems like an endless carpet of clustered and lumpy white floors. And this is where the stair to heaven ends. Breezie tests the ground with the tip of his shoe and finds firmness. All of us step out onto a ground surface made entirely out of clouds. The moment we are all with firm footing on heavenly grounds our stairs disappear.

"The surface is spongy and bouncy," Breezie says as usual walking ahead of us.

"What do you mean?" Asks Greenie.

"Let me check if it is what I think so I can show you guys what is about?" he says.

Breezie jumps in the air and lets himself drop to the ground flat on his back. To our surprise, the floor acts as a spring and Breezie bounces a good ten meters up. But it all happens as if in slow motion. Now he flips and summersaults. Then he back flips and rolls over in the air. Now he levitates while suspended ten meters high above. Soon we start to imitate him. Next, we all become 8-year-olds on a jumping bed with the difference being that this one is made entirely out of heavenly clouds.

The culminating point occurs when lateral clouds allow us to bounce laterally and zoom forward at almost ground level until we lose momentum, fall to the ground, just to spring up once more. We go about it, having fun until we tire.

"Meeting in the Clouds"

That's when within the cloud layer formation we see a small hut in the distance. With trepidation, we walk over the spongy surface towards it. The door is ajar when we get close to it. The eternally curious Greenie is the first one to peek. She immediately waves at us to do the same. What our six peeping heads find inside is pleasantly unexpected. The three characters that we met at different times during our visits through France to the six astrological clocks, my father's three mentors: Mrs. V., Mr. M., and Mr. N. are all inside.

"Welcome young wizards, come in, we've been expecting you," says Mr. M., taking the lead with his baritone voice and the crispiest of English accents.

We step in with trepidation and find six empty pupil desks waiting for us.

"Have a seat, please," says Mr. N. in a more formal tone. The three wizards contemplate us with benign eyes.

"The key question the three of us have about each one of you is simple," he adds.

"And it's whether you all deserve to become master wizards at this point?" Mr. N. asks.

"In other words, have you earned your credentials or not?" he says.

Tiny Mrs. V. stands up and starts pacing in short bouncy steps.

"Blunt, decades ago, having fulfilled our mission; one we had started when he was only eight years old, the three of us had a final mentoring session with your father; by then he was in his early twenties and had just finished his post-graduate studies at Harvard," she says.

Mr. N. remains seated as he follows Mrs. V's remarks, "in a way our encounter today is a final session as well. Though this time our responsibility is greater as there are six of you and we are not among mundane mortals. After all, you all are already young wizards and want to become master wizards," he. says in a formal fashion.

"A number of questions will be posed to you. They will show up as words floating in the air along with several possible answers; you will select and pair up a question with an answer you deem to be correct simply by touching both of them. You have to reply by yourself without any help from your peers. An accurate pair will turn green and an incorrect one will turn red. Any of you that fails to pair answers with questions three times will be eliminated," states Mr. M.

"Good luck young wizards," say the three mentors as they rapidly fade away.

We look at each other with anxious eyes. That's when the short floating sentences and possible answers start to appear; all the letters are bright white.

"Freedom lies within?" is the question that captures my attention.

'This question comes from one of the six books Mrs. V. gave us to read during our train rides between each of the astrological clocks,' I think for everyone to hear.

Hypnotized I raise my hand and "me," is the answer I select.

At that moment both the question and the answer start to flash while turning green.

"Blunt, how did you find out?" Greenie asks.

"It is part of the book called 'The Happiness Triangle'," I reply.

Checkered chooses the question, "What is perhaps the only state of continuous happiness?"

Decisively she chooses "Inspiration" and since the answer is right the words start to flash in green color.

This time it's Reddish who selects a question and an answer.

"What is the most elevated level of happiness?"

"Joy"

Once again an accurate pairing is rewarded with flashing green. We all look at each other in complicity; all three questions come from the same book.

"Why do you deserve to become a master wizard?" is the question Greenie selects.

"Because I have mastered every human virtue and flaw I was presented with and have completed the six challenges I faced as well," is the answer she selects and is correct as the words flash in green as well.

"How many crucial mistakes did you incur during the six challenges phase?" Firee selects it along with "Two" and again the reply flashing green confirms that is accurate.

"Which one was the most dangerous of the two?" is the follow-up Breezie selects and pairs with the reply, "The elevators," and is immediately rewarded with flashing green for accuracy.

"Are spells written or composed in Latin?" "They all can be but more important is the fact that they sound like if they are though," This time Greenie reacts faster than any of us, and to top it all, the flashing green letters confirm that her pairing was accurate.

"Why fix the Lyon clock with the makers of another clock?"

"Why not? What's wrong with that?" is the pair I select and the pairing is correct.

"What is the last freedom standing when everyone and everything has been lost?"

"Hope" is the reply Breezie chooses and is also rewarded with flashing green letters.

"What's the glue that connects meaning and purpose in life?"

"Coherence," is the pair Reddish chooses accurately, flashing green confirm that the selection is correct as well.

"We acclaim humanity and the creator with..?"

"Faith" is the pair flashing green the moment Checkered is done.

"What is the importance of the small details in life..?"

"That's how we conquer someone else's heart," says Checkered.

At that moment the stairs of heaven make themselves present again. Without hesitation, we start to descend following the same sinuous path.

"What was the point of what just happened. Simply to feel

what it really means to walk and bounce on clouds?" asks Greenie.

"I would say that what we've just experienced is the fact that being above clouds is something joyful and fun. Forever we will always associate it with happiness," says Reddish.

"I mean symbolically it means as well that to achieve happiness we have to pursue it, we have to climb, there has to be an effort to reach the clouds and somehow by reaching this elevated state we get closer to the creator," says Checkered.

The moment she finishes her statement, the steps underneath collapse into a slippery flat surface. We drop on our butts and begin to slide down. This time it's a gentle glide through elongated turns and a mild slope. We descend through clouds, and in the distance we soon begin to see the magnificent city of Paris underneath. As we get closer, the Eiffel Tower comes into focus. When we reach the end, the slide turns flat; so we simply step up into the tower. We are back at the same spot where we started, an open-air platform and 3/4 of the way up on the tower's stairs.

When we are about to begin climbing, right in front of us stands our antiquarian mentor Lettizia Dilletante, the statuesque Nordic beauty.

"How wonderful my dearest mentees. Congratulations, you've successfully completed your last challenge, the virtue of Tolerance. I believe you now understand very well the human virtue of tolerance. I wish you all the best in your endeavors. Now it's time for you to go and claim your credentials of master wizards; time is of the essence as your 24 hours are about to expire," she says blowing a kiss to us all and vanishing in an instant.

We hurry up the stairs and a short time later we reach the viewing platform at the very top of the tower. Right there wearing a broad smile stands the burly man, the human form of

The Orloj with Thumbpee seated on one of his shoulders and Buggie buzzing incessantly as his usual self.

"Welcome, welcome. Congratulations! You've all successfully completed this year's quest to become master wizards. Now if you'll be so kind to accompany me; we'll take a little stroll to a special place to grant you your official credentials as master wizards," the ancient time-keeping machine says as with one hand movement he swipes his arms creating a portal in the form of a small door. He then walks through it and filled with excitement while high-fiving each other, following the Orloj, we all walk right through what amounts to a thin wall of blurry air.

"Master Wizards Induction Ceremony, Palace of Versailles"

We are standing outside the magnificent palace of Versailles in the middle of its gargantuan garden.

"Before I induct you as master wizards, let me introduce you to what on next year's quest will be a new companion," the Orloj says.

To our shock, in addition to Thumbpee and Buggie suddenly, we now see a golden rooster cackling lying on the Orloj's other shoulder.

"Let me introduce you to my eldest son. He's normally the clock's hand that signals the European Central Time; on your next year's quest, he'll be joining my other two sons as your guide and companion. Believe me, you'll need the three of them," he says as he proceeds to give us our credentials as master wizards.

Yelling and screaming we jump up and down in joy and gratitude; we hug and kiss celebrating the feat and accomplishment to the joy and delight of the Orloj and his three kids. But we are not done yet.

Suddenly, we see in the sky above us, the images of three

women dressed in togas.

"Master wizards, let me introduce you to the three goddesses of fate - known as Moirai- in classical mythology. Their names are Clotho (the Spinner), Lachesis (the Allotter) and Atropos (the Inflexible). They decide the course of humanity. For next year's quest, which will take place in the United Kingdom primarily in the city of London, you'll have to decipher each one of the meanings of the riddle of fate before you begin your quest," says the ancient timekeeping machine wearing a big wide smile, while bowing and slowly fading away along with his small entourage.

Before we can even react and say goodbye to him, we start to feel the familiar dizziness; everything around us becoming blurry and in a void in time we are all transported back to the present. Slowly we begin to see the blurry images of my uncle Bartholomeous and my aunt Maria Antonella enjoying an animated conversation with Kraus on a stand next to the astrological clock of the French city of Ploermel, the exact place where we crossed Mr. Kraus' portal, which took us to the Notre-Dame Cathedral in Paris. When they see us, we know that our chaperones have a vague idea of what has happened to us in the last 24 hours, though to them is only a few minutes that have passed. Kraus is nowhere to be seen when both effusively hug each one of us.

"Welcome back master wizards," they say in tandem.

An hour later at the Gare de Lyon in Paris together with my aunt and uncle, we wave goodbye to my five mates and their respective parents.

As for me, I'm teary-eyed after hugging tight and seeing my uncle Bartholomeous off to Boston. I board a train bound to Milan alongside my aunt Maria Antonella on my way to fulfill the promise I made to her to spend time with my Italian cousins. Little do I know that my new master wizard status will soon after be put out to test throughout my Italian visit.

EPILOGUE

"The Central Institute of Arts and Literature"
(Fall 2057)

Professor Cromwell-Smith II and his students slowly come back from the trance they are in.

"Class, I wish you all an insanely awesome summer. Next semester I'll take you to the final Orloj adventure that took place exactly one year later in the city of London," says the eccentric pedagogue before loading his backpack on one shoulder and walking briskly off the stage wearing a still dreamy yet deeply satisfied expression.

As he approaches his bike, both earphones suddenly buzz registering an incoming call from his other half..

"Was any of it real?" Asks Lynn with a bemused tone.

"Not everything is what it seems around you, my love," the eccentric professor cryptically replies as he pedals away in direction to the California's Central Valley Hyperloop station.

Acknowledgment:

Special thanks to D. Suster, Elisa Arraiz, and Tracy-Ann Wynter. Your invaluable help and blind faith on my work have been an intrinsic part of the creation of The Orloj. Also, Daniel Dorse for his masterful work on The Equilibrist, and The Orloj series audio books. Thank you all.

9 781736 996874